Dwellers in the Mist

DWELLERS IN THE MIST

DWELLERS IN THE MIST

BY

NORMAN MACLEAN

NEW YORK   CHICAGO   TORONTO

FLEMING H. REVELL COMPANY

LONDON AND EDINBURGH

G. P.

New York : 158 Fifth Avenue
Chicago : 63 Washington Street
Toronto : 27 Richmond Street, W.
London : 21 Paternoster Square
Edinburgh : 30 St. Mary Street

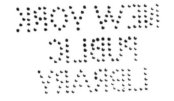

CONTENTS.

DILEAS

I

A LIGHT IN DARKNESS

IT was on a day of gray mist and weird shadows that Dileas came to the weather-beaten manse beside the sea. The rain clouds were trailing slowly through the glens, and the waves as they rolled lazily towards the land from a windless sea, and broke in white foam on the shore, had a prophecy of coming storm in their muffled roar. With the breaking of the storm, and the blotting out of the great world beyond in a deluging rain came Dileas, blending her little cry with the wild voices that rose and fell in ceaseless roar without. While yet her eyes were dim with the shadows of the mist they called her Dileas, for the word was dear to them; and from the first they would thus endow her with the fellowship of their own high ideal—they would have her grow up *faithful* to truth, to purity, and to God.

Her father was the minister of the gray church that stood on the hill overlooking the sea. Its walls were green with lichen, and its flooring was the damp clay in which the narrow, moth-eaten pews were fixed. Though it was erected but fifty years ago it was already far advanced in decay, for it was built in haste to provide a place of worship for the people who had then left the parish church in a body, leaving it empty and desolate. The old parish church stood near, and in it a kindly old man, known in the parish as the " Ministeir Moderate," ministered to a congregation so small that one of the qualities of the church triumphant might be claimed by it—for it was almost invisible. When the people wanted seed in the spring, or meal in the winter, they always went to the old minister in their need, and they never went in vain. That they should turn to him in their difficulties, while they would never dream of entering his church, seemed quite natural to them. Was he not there to care for their temporal needs?—and glad he was to have even that to do—while their own minister, whom they supported with much self-denial, cared for their spiritual needs. While the parish church was well-nigh empty, the gray church on the hill was filled by a congregation of stern and sturdy men, who won a precarious living from the deep, and looked on life with serious eyes.

How he came to be settled there as their minister was a wonder to all who knew William Macleod; his companions had prophesied in the old days that he would do great things. When he was moved none could speak with such fiery eloquence, and when he chose none could so easily master the deep thoughts of men. Though a Free Churchman to the core, yet in the city his favorite place of worship had been the old Cathedral, where he would sit under the tattered flags of dead soldiers, for he loved to hear the great organ " surge through arches dim," and to look at the storied windows through which the dim light fell on him, consecrated by the glowing pictures of the Man of Sorrows. These things never failed to touch his heart.

And now he was minister of a church whose walls were green with damp, in which a precentor with but one tune led the praise, where a cracked bell called the people to prayer, and where even the mention of a hymn or an organ would scare the congregation forever from his ministry. It was his duty to come there, he said. Ministers who could preach to the people in their own tongue were scarce. Good people had helped him through his studies for the very purpose that he might minister to such as these —and so, when the invitation came, he felt in honor bound to accept. He would not stay a very long time, he told himself; but once settled in a far-away place, remote from the centers of activity and thought, even the best of men are passed over and forgotten. Ten years have gone and he is still minister of a sea-washed promontory where steamers come

once a week, and he has become a dreamer of
dreams, a gazer at clouds, a listener to the
voices of the sea. Thither he brought his wife
from the great city; she would be there but a
little while, he told her; and 'mid his loneliness
she alone could cheer and comfort him. When
the little child came to them he was at rest.

On the long winter nights by his peat fire he
loved to bury himself in his books. Sometimes
it would be Gibbon, sometimes the ponderous
pages of Milman; but he would suddenly sit
up and listen eagerly when he heard the patter
of little feet along the long, flagged lobby
which led from his study to the back of the
windy manse. He knew well what followed—
the impatient tapping of little hands at the
closed door, the imperious childish cry, "Ope'
doo', Dada, ope' doo'"; the clambering up on
his knees, and the throwing away of his books
in obedience to the order, "Bookie away, Dada,
bookie away!" and the half-hour of perfect
contentment as he played hide and seek in the
dark corners where the shadows cast by the

glowing peats lay. The innocent prattle and the merry romp made him forget the bitterness that was eating into his heart, and his troubles with Eachann Donn, his stern elder, who suspected his orthodoxy, and whom he looked upon as his thorn in the flesh. Ah! what would he not give now as he sits by the fire thinking moodily of all that Eachann Donn has said and done, if he could hear again the eager rush of little feet along the long-flagged passage, and see the vision of golden curls and blue eyes with the look of the sea, and the mist in them, invading his dusky room, and hear the little voice cry, " Bookie away, Dada, bookie away! "

II

THE troubles which had been long brewing in the minister's congregation—those troubles over which he brooded many long nights—at last came to a head. They were not of his making. All over the Isles a spirit of restlessness had possessed the people. Strange rumors passed from township to township of strange doctrines and stranger laws which were being propounded by their Church—their own Church, to which they had given all their hearts. One day an old paper came to the parish, in which was a short account of a service held for the Scotch soldiers at York, when the pipers of the Cameron Highlanders took part in the praise. That paper went from house to house, and many a gray head wagged ominously in the peat reek over the degeneracy of the times.

Were there not organs in their churches in the south? Was there not even a thing which a man blew with his feet, and worked on with his hands, drawing out fearsome sounds in the church on the Meall at Port-a-Righ? Soon they would have Domhnull Cam, the piper, the ne'er-do-weel of the parish, supplanting old Murachadh, their precentor, with the one tune, who always explained apologetically that if he had not many tunes, yet that he sang with the spirit—and so he did! And were there not teachers who taught that there were errors in the Book—their only treasure—and some that said that God did not make Adam at all—only sea-worms which grew to be men? And their own minister—was he all sound? Did not the schoolmaster—for whose sake and for his own wife's he preached in English—say that he never heard a minister who could quote poetry so beautifully in the pulpit; what right had he to introduce any poetry save the holy Psalms into the pulpit? Truly he was not sound!

So they talked by their fires in the long

winter nights. What else had they to talk about? The ban of a deadly puritanism had been imposed on their lives by their own religious leaders. Music, dancing, and innocent games—all were under the one condemnation. What their fellow churchmen in the south laughed at was a matter of life and death to them. Children of the mist, driven to barren lands and rock-bound shores with naught to make life beautiful to them—they had only the Book. On it they anchored the hopes of eternity—it was their one comfort—if there were errors in it, might it not be all one error? Where then would be the one hope for which they lived?

It may seem strange to others that they should muse over these things till the fire of anger burned within them; but William Macleod was of their blood and he knew. He felt the chill which fell between him and his people. Each Sunday the sensitive man in the pulpit felt they were moving farther away from him. The knowledge was bitterness, heaped-up bit-

terness that he felt himself helpless.   But each
day as he turned sad and cheerless from his
church, the little child with the rippling, golden
curls met him at the rickety gate, and clasping
his hand, would say, " Ti'ed Dada, poo' Dada,"
and the clinging, tender fingers comforted
him.

Then it was that Eachann Donn waited on
his minister and spoke his mind.   He told him
that the people were waiting for him to speak
out against the backsliding and heresies of the
day; and he made it plain that unless this was
done the church would be left empty.   But
William Macleod was an honest man.   He was
there, he said, to preach the Gospel, and he
would not degrade his pulpit by entering on
useless controversies.

"It is my opinion," said Eachann, "that
you yourself do not believe in the doctrines of
election and eternal punishment.   It is long
since I waited to hear you preach on them, but
never a word you uttered.   These were the
truths on which we were nurtured; and I tell

you the people will not endure it unless you speak out on the evils of the day."

" Did you ever hear," asked Macleod, " what the saintly Leighton said to his Presbytery, three hundred years ago, when they found fault with him for not 'preaching to the times.' "

Eachann shook his head.

" ' Surely,' answered Leighton, ' you might permit a poor brother to preach Jesus Christ and eternity.' "

" Who was he? " asked Eachann, feeling a trifle abashed at the minister's learning.

" He was a bishop who——"

" A bishop. Was he? That is enough; I want to hear no more about him. They have all the mark of the Beast."

'And Eachann went out into the night.

When Eachann Donn went back to his thatched house, and told the tale, he declared that it was his own conviction that their own minister was as bad as any in the south. The leaders met, and they resolved to invite a deputation from the body which had already seceded, to visit them.

It was an early summer's day when the deputation came, and the crowd round the church on the hill was great. But the church was locked. When the key was asked for, it was refused. Then the wrath of the leaders broke out into white heat. Their own church that they had built with much self-denial, would they suffer themselves to be locked out? Was it for this that they left the bondage of the State Church fifty years ago? No! they would break in the door first! On the thatch of a house across the road there was an old mast; eager voices cried, "Let us ram in the door with the mast." Quickly the younger men ran for it, but ere they came back one got in at a window and opened the door, and in they poured, an excited throng waiting for the word that would settle their religious position for the future.

The meeting was remarkable, and they will long remember it. They sang with a peculiar wail, like the sea moaning round their own shores; and the sermon might have been preached at Drumclog. They heard in cool and measured tones of the backslidings of their Church. They heard more than enough to make them resolve never more to have part or parcel in the Church which they had loved so much.

Ere the service closed those who desired to separate themselves from the Church which had given itself over to evil ways and devious courses were asked to stand up. As one man they rose to their feet, with grim, resolute faces —all except Murachadh, the precentor, who could not tell why he did not stand up with the rest. Ere the shadows crept over the Isle that night, William Macleod knew that his day of trial had come.

III

SUNDAY was always a dull day for Dileas. There were no games with her father, no racing round the flower-beds in the garden, no walk with her mother over the moor to look for wild hyacinths. But there was one bright spot in the day; for it brought a crowd of people that went past the manse and turned in at the church gate. At the corner of the wall separating the garden from the church there was a gap in the bourtree hedge; and there the child used to stand on a stone so that her eyes looked over the wall, and, veiled by the foliage, watch the crowd streaming into the church—white-mutched old women leaning heavily on their sticks, young men and maidens who smiled to each other as they passed, and stern-faced, morose men, who wended their way into their

Father's house as if He had been a tyrant whom
they dreaded. When the Sunday after the
great meeting came, Dileas stole out as she
tried to do every Sunday. Sometimes she
failed to elude the watchful eyes of her mother;
but to-day she was successful. Her father was
left alone as usual till the hour of service, and
her mother was looking to the ways of her
household. So Dileas stood on the stone and
looked through the gap in the bourtree hedge
into the church ground, where the crowd used
to pass before her eyes into the open door.
But, alas! across the wall there was no sign
of life; the stream of life which had made it so
enticing to the child had deserted it. On the
road they passed in crowds, some talking loudly
and gesticulating eagerly; but none turned in
at the church gate. From where the child
stood she could not see the road on which the
people thronged past; she could only see the
path into the church, and it was deserted. 'A'
look of trouble crept into the eager little face;
why did not the people come in as before? why

did they all go past? She would go and ask
her father what it meant.

So she left the gap and ran across the sward,
carefully avoiding the narcissus, for which her
father lovingly cared; and through the open
door, and along the stone-flagged passage she
ran softly to her father's room. She looked at
him with troubled eyes.

"Oh, Dada!" she cried breathlessly, "I
stood at the gap to see the people go into the
church; but I can see none going into the
church. They are going past, all going past.
I stood long, long, and none turned in. Why
is it? Tell me, Dada."

He covered his face with one hand and
stroked her hair with the other.

"Run to your mother, girlie," he said
gently; "and do not ask questions."

Dileas turned and went out. She felt something was wrong. Her father had not even
rebuked her for standing in the gap of the
hedge on Sunday! Full of wonder she ran
again to the corner of the wall, and balancing

herself on the stone, she scanned the path into
the church. Perhaps the people would be
going in now. But the well-trodden path (the
grass is growing fast over it now!) was as
quiet as if it had been any other day but
Sunday; and outside the child could hear the
rush of feet hurrying to the big quarry where
a tent had been put up, though Dileas knew
it not. She waited patiently till at last the
church gate clicked, and old Murachadh, the
precentor and beadle, came up the path,
moving heavily. The child watched him
eagerly. He went into the church, but came
out immediately with his face clouded. The
church was empty. He looked at the old
cracked bell, and stood irresolute. The people
were all going past, what was the good of ringing it? Would it not be better to go with
them? He took a step towards the gate, and
then he stood again and looked at the bell. He
had rung it for so many years that his mind
got sore when he tried to count them. After
summoning the people to prayer through all

these years, was he to stop now? They would not come, but what of that? He would do his duty, and, at least, in the quarry when he stopped ringing, they would know it was time to begin the psalm. No other hands would ring it while he lived. Slowly and painfully he unknotted the weather-worn rope from the rusty hook in the wall and pulled. The bell sounded its harsh and grating note. The people thronging past heard, and looked up at the belfry. They smiled to each other and said, "Old Murachadh is not to be at the quarry"; but none turned in at the gate.

Surely now they will come, thought the child. The crowd along the path to the church door always grew bigger when Murachadh began to ring the bell. But soon the hope died within her, for still the people hurried past, and no foot fell on the path leading to the open door of the church. The eyes of the child grew wide with wonder. What had happened to the people—the nice women who used to pat her head and kiss her? The little mouth drooped; the lips quivered. She must run to her father again and ask. He would surely tell her now.

She treaded very gently as she passed her mother's room, and she softly opened the door of the study and went in. At the window she saw her father kneeling beside a chair, with his face towards the light. Dileas remembered then that her father, who was so tall, could see from the window the path leading into the church. He had seen it too, she thought; he was troubled by it. She ran up to him and put both her hands round his neck and held him tight as he knelt by the chair praying for strength to endure the desolation of that day. He rose and clasped her to his bosom.

" Why are 'oor eyes wet, Dada? " she asked, for she saw the tears glistening on his face. " The bell has been linging and nobody is come to the church—is that the cause, Dada? "

" Yes, that is it," he answered; " the people have gone away from me."

Again the little hands went round his neck—

oh! so tight—and the little mouth kissed him again and again, and the little voice cooed to him, "Neve' 'oo mind, Dada; Mamsie and Dileas have not left you. Mamsie and Dileas love you more than eve'. Neve' 'oo mind, Dada."

And he did not—at least not quite so much after that. Out at the church the rusty bell still jangled, and the people as they came up to the front of the church looked at it, and yet none turned in. At last the bell stopped, and Macleod went out to the vestry. In a little Murachadh came to the vestry as usual. Before the service the minister and the elders always prayed there together; Murachadh was the only one of them left, and Macleod asked him to pray. The old man had a gift of prayer. He knew little of life and less of the world; but by the sea and on the hillside he had communed with his God. It used to be a heartening thing to hear him pray. But now his tongue seemed tired. His heart was perhaps at the quarry. The old phrases could not be applied to an empty church. The voice of the old man quavered; he could only plead the promise to the two or three gathered in their Lord's name. That day they would be but two or three; but if they would only have His presence, the two or three would be better than 'thousands without that presence. So the old man plead while one or two passed into the church. The prayer ended, Macleod passed 'in to face the bitterest trial of his life.

The service began as usual. The psalm was given out, and Murachadh got up in his box below the pulpit to lead the praise. His hands 'holding the book were trembling. He knew only the half of a strange, wailing tune; but the people always carried it on, and when Murachadh faltered their voices rang out exulting in the glorious attributes of Him who was thronged on the clouds and veiled by the mists. But now there was no volume of voices to carry on the halting tune. The half-dozen who sat huddled together in a corner for the sake of companionship could not open their mouths.

The empty spaces silenced them. Murachadh's voice broke; he tried to recover himself, but his voice died away, and with a smothered groan the old man sat down and looked helplessly at the broken patch of ceiling at the back of the damp-stained church. The minister stood up in the pulpit and said with a steady voice, " Let us call on the name of the Lord," and the half-dozen of a congregation stood up to pray.

Till that day it was a delight to Macleod to preach. His spirit was the spirit of the poet; his eager eye quickly caught every motion that showed in the faces of the people. Their eyes inspired him. He rendered back to them in glowing words the yearnings, the aspirations, which came to him from their upturned faces. But now an empty church spread its mean, stained gray seatings before him; between the empty seats he could see the clay floor, where in crannies strange hart's-tongue ferns grew; the handful in a corner sat dejectedly with bowed heads. The fire and energy which came from a living congregation were gone. It was

only with an effort that he went on to speak
of Him who sat wearied at a wellside and
preached to one sinful woman. He had failed
at Jerusalem; the multitude had rejected him,
yet He did not despair. He knew the flood-
tide followed the ebb, and He preached the
Gospel of eternal consolation as earnestly to
the one as to the many. Thus with halting
words did Macleod, who formerly could stir the
hearts of the people as the west wind, coming
from the sea at eventide, stirs the cornfields,
speak of her who came aforetime to a well to
find water, and found a Saviour. As the service went on to its close his one thought was
that he must not break down as Murachadh
broke down. And he did not break down.
The tears were in his voice; the desolation of
the church in its naked ugliness, bereft of the
people, fell on him as a pall. But he went on
to the end and played the man.

IV

THE SHADOW OF DEATH

THE hour, however, was near when the minister would weep. A few weeks later as he went sadly home, Dileas, with the waving hair and the eyes with the mystical shadows in their blue depths, was not at the gate to meet him. Usually she burst out like a sunbeam through the gloom, lightening his heart; but to-day the gloom is unrelieved. Dileas was not well in the night; but she was better in the morning, and when he left she said, "Dileas meet 'oo at the gate, Dada"; but she was not there. He hurried in and found her ill indeed—she tossed, hot and feverish, her breath came hard and labored. All night they watched in hopes and fears, but when morning came she was not better.

The doctor lived fourteen miles away, and at

first they hesitated to send for him, the distance made the expense great, and it might be but a cold. Now they hesitated no longer; and when the gruff but kindly old man came and saw her he asked sternly why he was not sent for sooner, and muttered many awful words under his breath not fit for a minister to hear. He whispered to the father the dreadful word which blanched his cheeks—diphtheria—and he said he feared he was too late, and so it proved.

How William Macleod lived through the day and the night that followed he never knew. He, however, remembered how at the end the wearied, white face lined in the damp gold curls smote his heart like a sword in the flesh when he dared look at it; how each fluttering gasp for breath pulled at his heart-strings; how, after a few moments' sleep, she opened her eyes and saw him, and whispered, " Ti'ed, Dada, ti'ed," and closed them never to open again in this world; and more keenly than all, perhaps, he remembered how his wife, who bore it all unflinchingly till then, fell in a dead faint. Well for her, he thought, as he carried her out and laid her on her bed. Then he stumbled to his study where he had often played with his child. He sat before the grate, but he saw nothing, felt nothing; the world was one emptiness in which he groped with blind hands.

How long he sat there he could not tell, when suddenly there came a clear, loud tap on the window-pane. He started up, trembling with horror. What was it there tapping in the darkness at his window? A messenger from the dead! Ah! There, tap, tap on the highest pane it was again. He staggered to the closed shutters and opened them, but it was only the straggling branch of a Rambler rose caught by the gusts of wind that blew fresh from the sea driven against his window. The look of the sea and the land, as he saw them in that gray dawn, impressed his mind indelibly. He saw the waves with white crests tumbling on the shore, and away in the east he saw the clouds turning golden and red with long, fanlike streams of light rising upward over the hills, and as he turned from the dawn he realized it all. The grate before which he sat held a dead fire—a mere handful of gray peat ashes—and all his hopes were dead; and his golden-haired Dileas was dead; and his congregation, that was once living and warm at heart, was dead; and the waves as they washed backward from the shingly beach making the grinding pebbles moan—the weirdest sound in nature, he thought—seemed to echo Dead, Dead!

As the day advanced he felt that arrangements had to be made for laying the little one in her long home, but he could not rouse himself. His heart was full of a wild revolt against his lot. Then there came one to give him comfort—one that he never expected—the old parish minister. The two men, as they clasped hands, felt the thrill of a common sympathy—were not both their churches now well-nigh empty, only that of the young man more so? Forty years of solitude do not produce facility of speech, and the old minister said little as he sat beside the stricken man who,

however, felt the unspoken sympathy and knew
it good.

After a long silence the old minister asked
if he might pray, and the two knelt together
there, pouring out their hearts before God.
Macleod never forgot that prayer; its yearning,
pleading tones fell on his heart like healing
balm.   When he heard the petitions—" May
they realize in their sorrow how tender the
Hand is which wipeth away the tears from
their eyes; may they believe that their little one
is better with Thee than with them; better in
Thy house of glory, where sin and sorrow are
not, than on earth, where sin and sorrow and
death are.   May they be taught to say ' the
Lord gave and the Lord hath taken away,
blessed be the name of the Lord ' "—the heart-
broken man said Amen in his heart, and rose up
strengthened for the duties that remained.
He had one feeling as he thought of the child's
burial, and that was that he could not place her
in the parish graveyard, which lay on a hill
round a ruined chapel of the old faith.   The

site was most beautiful. These old builders
knew where to plant their churches. The
Minch shimmered before it and wailed around
it; a stream sang near it, and green fields
stretched behind it. But there was none to
care for the little God's acre; nettles and weeds
grew rank in it; cattle strayed among the
graves, and rabbits burrowed in them. Round
his own church there was a well-walled plot of
green grass which he himself had beautified
with daffodils. He resolved to lay the little
one there, that he might look on her grave as
he passed in to prayer.

Thus he arranged; but with the next day
came to the manse old Murachadh, his precentor and elder—the only office-bearer left to him
—who asked where the child was to be buried.
When the minister explained his intentions
old Murachadh straightened his back, and said,
with a stern voice, that now he was the only
trustee left in the congregation, and that he
would not allow the child to be buried at the
church. She must be laid where all the parish

laid their dead. Was she different from others that she should need a place all to herself? "We always knew," he said, with unconscious brutality, "that you were not as other men; but I never thought you would seek to do so foolish a thing as this." And so he left. It was then that the minister's cup of humiliation and bitterness ran over. He bowed his head on the table and moaned, "How long, O Lord, how long!"

.   .   .   .   .

Now he has no desire to leave the wave-washed, lonely parish where he has suffered so much. He is anchored to it by a grave in the old churchyard, where the wind from the sea blows through the nettles and the weeds. That one little grave is always green with flowers around it. His wife prays that he may yet be called to a place where happiness might come to him again, but he has ceased to wish it. In the moldering church he preaches to a dozen people, but he sees them not, for often his face shines as he pictures in living words the beauty of the Shepherd who carries the lambs in His bosom, and his hearers feel that he is looking far beyond them, on the invisible. His wife's heart throbs as she listens, and she feels convinced that his merits must win him a place. How can they? The great world knows nothing of that lone land with its sad, other-world people. But she never despairs; she is certain a " Call " will come; and perhaps it will—too late!

V

BROTHERS IN ADVERSITY

In the dark season which followed, a close friendship sprang up between William Macleod and Dr. Macqueen, the old parish minister. In former days Macleod's feelings towards the Doctor were mixed; he respected him for his stores of lore and out-of-the-way learning, while he despised him not a little for devoting to these things the talents which, in another sphere, might have been applied to the noblest of all work—the saving of men's souls. Macqueen, for his part, was so engrossed in his own pursuits that he did not seek the companionship of the younger man. While Macleod had the people to minister to, their sympathy to uphold him, and their praises to cheer him; while he had wife and child to make his home happy for him, what more could he

need? Macqueen had neither a congregation,
wife, or child, but he lived his life neverthe-
less. He walked the moors at the flood-tide,
looking for strange plants; and at the ebb-tide
he paced the strand, watching the multitudinous
life of the shore. The life of the old minister
was twofold. In Dunaluin he was the " Ministeir Moderate "—as a minister of no account
whatever, but a kind, open-handed man who
never sent the needy away empty. In the
great world beyond the narrow Kyles, his name
was better known than that of any in the Isles.
His contributions to papers and magazines on
shore life and moor life, on rats and insects,
on witchcraft and spells brought him fame and
friends. When his university honored him
with the degree of Doctor Dunaluin wondered
greatly. If Macleod had been thus honored
they would have understood it; but Macqueen
knew more about beetles than about justification by faith, and could talk more readily about
Ossian than about the Bible; and there was
more in his sermons about moths and peri-

winkles and such things than about the great doctrine of election—at least so Domhnull Cam declared after going once to hear him preach. Seumas Ban, the post, was the one man in Dunaluin who had a great admiration for the old Doctor: "Dr. Macqueen gets more letters in a week than anybody else in the parish does in a whole year"—that was the way Seumas used to give vent to his sense of the Doctor's greatness.

But when the days of trouble came to Macleod, he found in Macqueen a friend. When the long winter set in, Macqueen often made his way to the neighboring manse to sit and smoke with Macleod in his study. Out of respect to Macleod's wife the Doctor always put on his velvet coat—a coat which he only donned on great occasions. Jean welcomed these visits, for her husband had of late grown morose and silent, and would sit whole evenings without speaking. If he heard any sound along the passage he used to turn eagerly to the door, as if expecting Dileas to burst into the room as

of old, and then he would go and lift the blind
and look out at the window, as if he wanted to
see how the weather was promising. Macqueen, however, never failed to rouse him in
some way. While the two men smoked (the
Doctor compelled his companion to fill his
pipe), and Jean sat silent, knitting, Macqueen
talked, as he only did on rare occasions, of
books and *sgeulachdan* and the strange fancies
of untutored minds, and he never failed to
evoke a smile from his companion. For that
smile Jean grew grateful to Macqueen.

One evening when Macleod was even more
silent than usual, Macqueen said quietly:

"You must rouse yourself, Macleod, and do
something, or you will soon be useless."

"What can I do?" replied the other. "The
only thing I gave my heart to was preaching,
and now that is lost to me. No man can preach
without a congregation of some kind."

"There are scores of things you can do,"
said Macqueen. "There's the varied life in
the fields, and you hardly know one plant from

another; go and study them.   One pool in the
shore is a world by itself, swarming with life
and color.   There are the rocks which interpret
the past to the present.   Men speak of the
country as dull; it is the stone walls and pave-
ments of towns with no life but sordid human-
ity that are dull.   Here we are surrounded
with glowing life waiting to enrich our lives
with its beauty and mystery.   When I came
here young, and found that the inner lives of
the people were shut against me, and I had
nothing to do, I began to study insects—a wonderful form of life.   You get interested at
once.   When you watch them and see their
antennæ at times smelling, at times caressing
and making love, at times conveying their
thoughts to their fellows, you learn that men
are poor things after all.   Why, you have only
to begin, and you will soon say, ' The more I
know of cockroaches the less I think of men.' "

Macleod smiled at the old man riding his
hobby.

"I cannot interest myself even in cockroaches," he said, " so long as this bitterness is eating my heart."

" Why should you be bitter? " asked Macqueen quickly. " When I found an empty church here, I did not allow myself to grow bitter. I knew it was not my fault. And that your church is now empty is not your fault."

" Ah! but the people for whom I toiled, and whom I loved, have forsaken me," replied Macleod. " They never forsook you; you cannot know the bitterness of it."

" That they left you was only an accident," continued Maqueen. " What they left was the Church to which you belonged. And they left it because they thought the Church threw doubt on the truthfulness of the Bible. The common mind must have something infallible to rest on—an infallible church or an infallible book. We only exchanged the latter for the former at the great upheaval. You did not throw these doubts on the Book—others did. Their Bible is all their treasure. It is life and hope and comfort to them. They are content clinging to their barren patches of rain-sodden soil, listening to the moan and coronach of the sea, because their eyes are on the Invisible. But if the Book be not infallible, may it not be all one delusion, and then where is the hope for their lost lives? What wonder that in a mood of blind rebellion they throw over Church and minister to cling to that hope—the hope of the world invisible, based on an infallible book. Why, you had nothing to do with their leaving the church. You are not to blame."

"I know how they feel," said Macleod. "My heart said, 'Go with them,' but my reason said, 'Stay where you are.' Perhaps I would be happier if I obeyed my heart."

"No, you wouldn't," exclaimed the old man; "for you would not be honest, had you gone contrary to your own convictions. After all, it is foolish to blame the people. You can distinguish between Revelation and the channel of that Revelation, and can see that imperfection in the channel does not affect the reality of Revelation; but how can the people realize that?

If Revelation were denied by the Church, you would go out too; and so far as they see it, the truth of a Revelation from God is denied. Besides, they have left you the church while they have shut other ministers out. That shows that they love and respect you as a man."

"But I would prefer if they had shut the church door against me," replied Macleod slowly. "They built it with their life-blood, and they worship in the open air, and I in the empty church. I would be happier if I saw the crowd turning in at the church gate as of old, even though I preached in a hut. As it is, they make me feel as if they were martyrs. I would hand over the church to-morrow if I had the power. Empty walls do not make a church."

The eyes of the old man shone.

"If I were you," he said, "I would only remember that they did not disturb me in possession of their church. That shows their regard."

VI

THE GREAT MYSTERY

ONE night when the two men were alone,
Macleod startled the old minister by asking
suddenly:

"Do you believe that we live after death?
I want you to tell me your inmost opinion, not
what you would like to believe, or what would
help one to believe, but your honest conviction."

Macleod's face was drawn; the suddenness
of the question showed that it was with an
effort he asked it. Macqueen was so much
taken aback that his pipe fell from his mouth
and broke on the hearthstone. If he had been
asked, "Do you believe in Ossian?" he would
have answered volubly and convincingly, and
answered at once. If an insect had been produced and its name asked, he would have

answered at once—one of the species Cole-
optera, genus Menognatha, and he would have
discoursed on it for an hour. But to be bluntly
asked, " Do you believe in life after death? "—
that was quite another question. He must gain
a little time to think. His lore of entomology
had no answer to that question, behind which
lay the silent cry, " Does my child live? "

" Why do you ask that? " he replied at last.
" I never dreamt you could doubt it for a
moment."

" And neither I did," said Macleod; " not till
these last months. When my life was full of
work, and a crowd hung on my lips for comfort
and help, it was easy to believe the truths I
preached. But now that things have gone
wrong, the empty church is killing my
faith."

" And my church has been empty these forty
years," murmured the old man, " and yet he
asks *me*."

" When we see the religion of peace bringing strife," continued Macleod, " and bearing

the fruit of bitterness and ill-will instead of
love and charity, may it not be all a mistake?
Perhaps we have been hugging an illusion these
nineteen hundred years."

The old man gazed at the glowing peats, and
remained silent.

"Last night," went on Macleod, "I went out
to look at the sea in the starlight, and when I
looked upward to the heavens the sense of the
littleness of human life came over me in a
flash. It was all so easy in the ancient days,
when this world was supposed to be the center
of the universe, with the sun and the stars
moving round it, to believe that men, the crown
of the world, were too important to die. But
now the humiliating knowledge cannot be
evaded, that the world is only a fifth-rate
satellite of a fifth-rate sun. I looked up at
Sirius—it glowed in Orion as I never saw it
glow before—and I remembered what I read
long ago, that it was twenty times greater than
the sun, and I thought how, unseen by us,
worlds revolved round it; and how each star in

the great vault above me was a sun, the pivot
of a system of worlds. What was this little
earth among them all, as one grain of sand to
all the sand in the world. And I remembered
that if this world of ours were consumed with
fervent heat, and passed away leaving no trace,
the dwellers in the planets revolving round
Sirius would never even know that such a
catastrophe happened, because the earth is so
small that they cannot see it, even had they
telescopes as we have; and that if the sun itself
and all the planets perished, all they would
notice was that one small star stopped
twinkling in that myriad of stars which make
up the Milky Way. The whole earth might
perish, and yet in the abysses of space, 'mid the
systems and constellations of Omnipotence, its
loss would not even be noticed. The question
came to me there in the silence of the night;
a whole world might disappear unmarked in
the infinitude of creation, and do you think that
your petty life cannot disappear or perish?
Oh! the pettiness of it, the littleness and vanity

of it; how dare we believe that such a trifle is immortal!"

The old man gazed at the dim-glowing embers and remained silent.

"And then I remembered," continued Macleod, "how on this ant-heap of a world thousands of generations have lived and died—myriads of half-brutish, pre-historic men; myriads of Hottentots and fetich-worshipers; myriads of men who grappled with the overpowering darkness of a mysterious world—and all perished. What is our little life among those? Where are they? Gone as the leaves that fell in autumn. The human life is as nothing, and yet how do we think that it must necessarily survive 'mid the sway of all-devouring death?"

And still the old man gazed at the growing heap of gray ashes, and remained silent.

"And there was our little child," began Macleod again, with a choking voice (he had never spoken of her before), "the light of our eyes, and the sunbeam in our home, and yet

God struck her down, and made her bed where the sunbeams can never reach her, and left our house to us desolate. If she is dead, and we can never see her again, why, then, He is not a God I can serve or love. What do you say, Macqueen? Do you think she is alive?"

Then Macqueen found his voice and spoke at last.

"I too have felt like that," he said slowly. "The fruitlessness of preaching to emptiness almost killed my faith. But in time I saw the foolishness of blaming Christianity for men's perversion of it. It is not religion which creates strife and bitterness, but the evil in man for a time overcoming the spirit of love and peace. And I believe in life after death to-day with a stronger faith than ever. You forget that in the sight of God there is no such distinction as great and small. He alone is great. As for the rest, the wing of a butterfly is as perfectly formed as the orbit of a world, and both are alike before Him. What is great may not be valuable; what is very small may be most precious. The stars moving in their courses are vast; but the life of a little child may be more precious. Can a star love God? can a constellation commune with Him? can He in the hosts of heaven see the reflection of His glory—which is love? The human soul alone can commune with and love God, and as such is infinitely more valuable than a star."

"I did not think of that," said Macleod, with the shadow rising off his face.

"Aye, and those multitudes that perished on the earth, those brutalized men and women," went on Macqueen, "we can't think why they should go on living. We can't feel any interest in them. But they themselves thrilled with life, and God's interest in them cannot be exhausted. We cannot see any use for them, but He can. He is all-wise; and the All-wise does not create merely for the pleasure of destroying. I cannot think that the six feet of earth holds all that there is of a man when he goes hence. He must live."

" And you firmly believe that? " asked Macleod.

" Yes, I do," said Macqueen. " The Allgood does not create the bud of a living soul only to blast it."

The shadows were not so heavy on Macleod after that night. When Macqueen was gone, he said to his wife, " I never dreamed Macqueen was such a good man."

And Macqueen stood on his way home and looked up to the belt of Orion, and the shining pathway of the Milky Way. He took off his hat as he gazed on the mighty vault where the endless suns shone, merely as flickering points of light, till the sense of the infinitude of the creation seemed to lift him off his feet and cast him into the void.

" Was I right after all? " he asked.

" God is good, and I was right," he answered himself after a while.

" And what curs we are," he said to himself as he put on his hat and moved home to his lonely house, " to go on making this little

globule of a world the warring place of our
ambitions, the battlefield of our creeds, as if
we, who are but ants on an ant-hill, were Lords
of the Universe."

As he was opening his door to get in out of
the night, he muttered to himself:

"Aye," he said, "the more I know of men,
the more I think of cockroaches."

VII

IT was on a golden autumn day, when light
breezes ruffled the Minch and rustled through
the corn-plots that sloped down to the sea, that
the minister stood at his gate gazing on the
sun-bathed scene.   Mingling with the whisper-
ing of the corn, he heard the song of the women
that cut it down, and the whir of their reaping
hooks.   He was waiting for Seumas Ban, the
post, who soon appeared round the bend of the
road, whistling as he came.   Among the papers
that were handed to the minister was a letter
addressed in a unfamiliar hand-writing, and
this he opened first.   It was the letter for
which William Macleod had waited for eleven
years—an invitation to preach before the congregation in Glendessary, far away on the
mainland, with a view to his being elected as

their minister. "We have been recommended
by the leaders of the Church to invite you to
preach before us," the writer said, "and if you
can come and conduct services here on an early
Sabbath, we will be enabled to consider what
further steps to take." The letter fell from the
minister's hands, and he looked towards the
reapers and the rows of stooks, and the great
sea that lay bathed in the glorious light beyond,
but he saw them not. The eleven years of his
loneliness and struggle passed before him in a
flash. He saw himself as he came, full of
noble yearnings and high ideals, taking up his
like work, determined to offer to God the best
he was capable of; he remembered the keen
joy that was his when he brought to the crumbling manse his clinging bride from the city—
how proud he was of her! and how he laughed
when he overheard Domhnull Cam saying to a
neighbor that he wondered how their minister
ever had the face to ask her to marry him!
He recalled the little child that came to them
to lighten their somber lives with smiles and

laughter—and now she was dead! He felt again the shadows falling between him and his people, till at last his church was empty. The letter which lay at his feet opened all the old wounds, and the minister winced as he leaned against the gate. He had yearned for an escape from his unbearable position, but now that the way seemed open he did not feel that he could go. He had not been out of the Isle for years, and now he felt it would be misery to meet strangers. It seemed as if he could hear people whisper to each other as they pointed to him, " That is the minister who emptied his church." Better to stay where he was! In time he would become as contented as the old parish minister who, having no flock, devoted his time to many hobbies. With a smile he thought of the bottle in the old man's garden which he had fixed there as a rain gauge, and how the mischievous boys poured an inch of water into it each time the minister went from home, with the result that the parish boasted the heaviest rainfall in the kingdom.

He pictured himself soon falling heir to the old man in these pursuits—would that not be better than facing the ordeal of preaching to the strange people of Glendessary? No! he would not go.

And he would not, if his wife had not arranged it otherwise. When she read the letter she saw the gate, which had been so long shut, opened at last—the gate which might lead to renewed life and happiness for her husband. She spoke as if he could have no thought but when to start! With loving care she prepared him for his journey, and talked to him of the days that were—of the half-forgotten ambitions of youth, of the joys of a congregation that would inspire their minister, of the achievements of other days, when his comrades were often thrilled with his fiery speech—till he caught her enthusiasm and became eager to press through the door of escape that seemed open at last.

The church at Glendessary was crowded when Macleod came to preach. In the vestry, when he heard the organist begin the voluntary, his heart sank within him. The vision of a handful of people crouching in a corner of the desolate church at home rose before him. It was with faltering steps that he followed the beadle as he led the way to the pulpit. When he rose to give out the opening psalm the hundreds of curious eyes fixed on him seemed to take his strength from him. His voice seemed strange to himself. He had used the Gaelic language so much for these many years, that now in his nervousness he seemed to forget the language he was to preach in. The service was a disastrous failure. Few heard what was said, and the few that heard did not understand, for he could not think or recall his line of reasoning. In an agony of distress and humiliation he made his way to his lodging; and the burden of the people's conversation as they dispersed was that the minister who had preached that day would never do for them.

But he was to preach again in the evening,

and as he thought of his wife, who had been his stay 'mid his troubles, far away in her loneliness, and of the pain his failure would cause her, he braced himself for another effort. He would show these people that he was a man. Surely he could yet face his fellow-men unafraid! And when he stood in the pulpit for the closing service of the day he faced a much smaller congregation, but he was master of himself.

The people of Glendessary remembered that service for many years. His voice as he prayed thrilled with emotion. The farmer at Carn Ban, who had lost his son, felt that the minister was praying for him when he prayed for fathers and mothers who weep their dead, that God might show them their loved ones beholding the face of their Father.

The sermon was on the loneliness of Christ. Out of the fullness of his own heart he pictured to them the loneliness of the Man of Sorrows. Lonely! for he was in a world which understood him not. He pictured that loneliness as

of one alone on the sea where the waters of
separation flowed round him, so that none
could say, " I will cross over to his side; I will
share his solitude." And when he spoke of
the sea he pictured its wondrous beauty, its
endless charm, its never-ceasing wail, and the
lonely spirit in the midst of it, so that these
dwellers in an inland dale seemed as if they
heard the waves beat on the shore.

When the service ended Macleod was
waited on in the vestry by all the office-bearers,
and they informed him that he might consider
himself elected minister of Glendessary.

It was the man as he was years before who
returned to his wife on the following day.
She had spent the Sunday in an agony of sus-
pense. And now he came back with a look
of other days in his eyes, she knew at a glance
that all was well. When he told his tale they
sat hand in hand before the fire, and when the
minister felt a tear fall on his hand he knew
his wife was thinking of the little grave they
would now leave behind in the rabbit-burrowed

churchyard with none to tend it. In that sad
Isle, over which the clouds of a darkening
theology have fallen, there was none who would
keep green the grave in which the love of two
hearts lay buried.

VIII

BESIDE the sea in a miserable hut there lived
an old man and his aged sister. The sister's
limbs were so twisted with rheumatism that she
could only crawl about the house; and the
burden of the work thus fell on Ian Dubh, as
the brother was called. Their house was
among the worst of its kind. It was built
against a steep brae, so that from behind it
looked as if the thatch rose from the ground.
This mode of building saved a full wall at the
back of the house; but the rain gathered by
the hill oozed in through the rough stones, and
made the place damp and unwholesome. The
cattle occupied one end of the house, using the
same door with their owners. The peat fire
that burned on raised stones in the center of
the inner room filled all the place with reek.

There was no chimney and no window, save
one pane of glass fixed in the thatch. Ian
Dubh had lived there all his years, and he had
only seen a doctor once; nor did he want to
see one again. Some years before Ian Dubh
was ill, and he wrote the doctor asking that
medicine be sent to cure him. A reply came
that no medicine could be sent until the doctor
saw him first. But Ian was not to be beat.
He sent an old faded photograph of himself,
taken many years ago, when he had made a
journey to Glasgow, and told the doctor that
now, having seen from the photograph what he
was like, he must send on the medicine at once.
But the doctor was obdurate, and wrote again
that he must see Ian first. So the old man got
a cart and went to the doctor's house; but when
the doctor began to question him about his
ailments, Ian's one answer to every question
was—" It is you who art the doctor." The old
islander thought a doctor was an omniscient
person who, at a glance, ought to see what
ailed his patients, and that if he could not, then

he was of very little use. The doctor and his
patient parted without any mutual good will,
and Ian always chuckled when he told the tale.

But at last Ian Dubh was seized with sore
illness, and on the morrow after his return
home word came to the minister that the old
man would like to see him. When Macleod
came to the door, where a pool of green,
noisome water lay, and made his way through
the byre over a heap of rotting manure thinly
covered with straw, he felt as if he had fallen
from the light into utter darkness. In a box-
bed in a dark corner, where the light never
reached him, he found Ian Dubh, hot and
fevered, and rambling in his speech. It was
of the shoals of herrings on the bank, of the
boats sailing out with the nets, of the silvery
stream of fish falling below the thwarts at the
early dawn, that he talked. By the light of a
candle set in a bottle (though the autumn sun
glowed on the sea) he looked at the gray-
headed man, who tossed and muttered unceasingly. On his breast were the unmistakable

signs of fever. The minister knew it well, for in these foul houses it found its fit breeding place. The doctor was at once summoned, and when he came he pronounced it fever of a virulent kind; and then the awfulness of complete isolation fell on the house where the crippled woman strove bravely to tend the stricken man.

Only an islander can realize the frenzy of terror which possesses the township when fever breaks out in their midst. No helping hand is stretched out to the sufferers; no kindly neighbors come to their aid; they are left as if they were alone in the wide world. Brother has been known to desert brother; parents have even fled from their own children; and the one thought of all the people is to escape the dread thing. The poor man who was fighting for his life had only his well-nigh helpless sister, and she could do little. Macleod could not leave him to die like a dog, for the sister could not watch day and night, and he came to their help He tended the dying man with the

tenderness of a woman.   He brought the water
from the well; he gave the medicine the doctor
sent, for otherwise it would not have been
given; and part of every night he watched the
grim struggle between life and death while the
sister slept.   The unequal contest at last ended,
and in the chill midnight Ian Dubh set out to
sea.   For him there were no more treacher-
ous currents and baffling headwinds and nights
of rain, for his soul had launched out on the
great ocean of Eternity.   The sister composed
the dead man's limbs, and the minister waited
till the daylight dawned without, for in her
terror she dared not stay alone in the dark with
the dead.

After a day had passed a few neighbors
brought a coffin and placed it near the door,
that they might carry the dead man to his rest-
ing-place on the hill.   When the minister came
they stood there; but the coffin was yet empty,
and none would go in to bring out the dead.
The old woman could not, and they in their
blind terror would not.   Leaving them, the

minister went in; but he could not alone carry out the body.   They passed in a rope, the sister tied it round her dead brother; then they dragged out the body, the minister guiding it. Out of the darkness it came, feet foremost, through the door, and a young man in the little group, as he saw the naked feet creeping into the light out of the darkness within, while the rope was being slowly pulled, uttered a cry of horror; and on the pale set face of the minister was a look of anguish and shame which no cry could utter or relieve.   When the awful burden was dragged to the side of the black box those who pulled the rope let it drop; and the minister, nerving himself to the effort, lifted poor Ian Dubh into his last earthly shelter. The lid, which had been well tarred, was laid on it, and then one braver than the rest came forward and nailed it down.   Then they lifted it on a cart, and followed it afar to the hill where their dead were laid; but William Macleod walked close behind.

   "He is a brave man and a good," said

Domhnull Cam to Eachann Donn, as they walked far behind, " or he would not have done what he did to poor Ian Dubh. I am thinking we did not treat him well."

" He may be a brave man," said Eachann, " though for my part I would say he is not brave, but foolhardy. As to his goodness, that's another matter. He cannot be a good man, for he has no principles. If the fountain be impure, how can the stream be clean? He stayed in a church which everybody knows has no right principles—how then can he be a good man? Give me a man with right principles, say I."

Domhnull Cam was the parish's ecclesiastical outlaw—he played the pipes! And he looked at the minister with eyes full of admiration, and slowly answered, " You have good principles, have you, Eachann?—and he has none. What have your good principles ever done? Have you risked your life for your neighbor as he has done; or visited the needy and helped the helpless as he has done? I tell you what,

Eachann, I would rather be in hell with such as he than in heaven with such as you and your principles!"

Domhnull Cam never again sought the ministrations of Eachann Donn.

But as the little band turned home after filling up the narrow, shallow grave where Ian Dubh sleeps well in the hearing of the sea, they said one to another that the minister was a brave and kind man—but, then, what was the good of these natural virtues, for he lacked the foundation of all true godliness—he had no right principles!

IX

THE CALL

THE next day was Sunday—Sabbath they always call it—and when the minister awoke he had a violent headache. He carefully hid that from his wife, for he had never missed his Sunday service, and he was determined not to miss it that day. When at noon he went to his church there was not even one to meet him. He could always count on a dozen; to-day there was none. The panic had seized them; the dread he might carry the infection to all in the church had possessed them. He was isolated from his kind, for he had tended the man who was dead, and laid him in his coffin. The minister went into his pulpit. He saw the green walls, the broken plaster ceiling, the empty hideous pews, the crumbling house of prayer in which he had preached to living souls

who had forsaken him, and he bowed his head
and prayed. After an hour his wife followed
him, and she found him in an empty church
where no life was save a robin which fluttered
in through one of the broken windows, and he
was preaching with great earnestness while his
eyes shone with a strange light. She called
him, but he answered not; she ran up to him
and touched him, and he looked at her as one
in a dream. The fever had mastered him.
Supporting him with one hand she led him out
from the church where he had preached at last
to emptiness and air.

All that night till the gray dawn his mind
wandered unceasingly 'mid the days that were
no more. He sang snatches of old student
songs; he delivered fragments of speeches
before his college societies; but most awful of
all in the ears of his wife were the cries of half-
smothered laughter when he fancied himself
playing again with his child—his golden-
haired Dileas—in the dusky study.

As the crippled woman was left alone to

watch her dying brother, so now was she left alone to watch her husband. The doctor came as often as he could across the fourteen miles of moorland, and watched while she slept. Every day Domhnull Cam carried pails of fresh water from the well to her door, and laid beside them offerings of sweet milk and fish; and though he would come no nearer, she blessed him in her heart. The weary days passed and the crisis came, but the worn-out, heart-broken man—the dreamer of dreams, who could not mold events, but waited on them—had no strength to rally. In the early morning he awoke to consciousness, and saw the face of his wife beside him. He whispered to her, asking the hour.

"One o'clock," she answered, rejoicing that he knew her.

"Look out and tell me how the tide is," he murmured again.

She went to the window and looked.

"It is ebbing," she said; "about an hour from full ebb."

"What is it like?" he asked, speaking slowly and with difficulty.

"A three-quarter moon on the wane is moving westward," she said, "and there is a broad pathway of silvery sheen across the Sound; the wind is low and rippling on the sea, and the waves are stirring the palm-leaved tangles on the rocks; it is very beautiful."

"Death comes oftenest at the low ebb," he said with effort. "Oh, Jean, put your hand in mine and tell me you forgive me for the years of misery and loneliness I brought on you."

"They were not lonely," she answered between her sobs, "for I had *you*. And they were not miserable, for we shared their sorrows together."

And she laid her head beside his and kissed him.

And he fell asleep—a sleep gentle as a child's, so soft and gentle that she had to strain her ears to hear him breathe. Once he murmured in his sleep, "Oh, Dileas, I see you; I am coming"; and when the day was well-nigh bright, and all the reaches of the shore stirred with the wind through the sea-wave, the *call* came to William Macleod, and he found his golden-haired child again.

.   .   .   .   .

They buried him beside his child, where the ruined chapel casts its shadow over his grave when the sun is sinking behind the Uist Hills, and the eddying Minch gleams with myriad gems.   On the day they bore him forth Seumas Ban brought a letter and laid it under a stone on the wall at the gate, and blew his whistle to show it was there.   When the widow found heart to take it in and open it, she read through blinding tears that the congregation of Glendessary had unanimously elected William Macleod as the minister.

"Too late! too late!" she moaned in her misery.

THE WOMAN WHO NEVER
QUARRELED

THE WÔMAN WHO NEVER QUARRELED

MURACHADH, the elder, was a man of much repute everywhere in Dunaluin; but in his own house he played a part much inferior to Peggie his wife. Their house was one of the queerest in all the parish. It had been built by some ambitious man when the fashion of building chimneys in thatched houses had crept across the Kyles, and the house had two stone-and-lime chimneys. But Murachadh was not a man who cherished social ambitions, and when he entered into possession, the chimneys found no favor in his eyes. A peat fire in a cavity sunk into the gable end of a house had no charm for Murachadh. It was but a cold, cheerless thing; only three persons could sit at it comfortably. The old way was better. Round the fire glowing on a stone hearth in the center of the clay floor, a dozen could sit at ease with

their feet stretched towards the red embers—
a magic circle with a pillar of smoke rising
from the heart of lambent flames. It was when
men gathered round such fires that the good
tales were told in the days of old. For a few
days Murachadh endured the fire in the chimney hearth, and then he might be seen one day
climbing the roof of the house with large
heather divots, which he placed carefully on the
heads of both his chimneys, closing them effect-
ively. In the ridge of the roof he opened a
hole through the thatch and inserted in it an
oblong, square, hollow, wooden frame which
he had made, and tied it there with heather
ropes, giving it a slant westward. The former
hearth in the chimney he made the receptacle
of various boxes and bags, and on a slab of
smooth stone set as nearly as possible in the
center of his clay floor, right below the square
wooden smoke tube in the ridge, he lit his peat
fire as his fathers had done ever since the days
when they emerged from the caves and learned
to twist heather ropes wherewith to bind the

thatch on their huts. The following night when the neighbors came in to see Murachadh, he received them with great cordiality. They could be comfortable now as their fathers had been before them, with room for at least twenty-four feet on that capacious, circular hearthstone. And the neighbors congratulated Murachadh.

There were some, however, who insisted that it was Peggie who caused the chimney heads to be sealed with the heather divots. At any rate, sealed they were; and the stranger wondered as he passed and saw two chimneys fresh and smokeless, while the reek ascended through the wooden tube that sloped westward. And there is this to be said for these malicious persons who traced the mind of Peggie in the divot-crowned chimneys—it was she and not Murachadh who was the ruling power in the house. In fact, there was no man more helpless than Murachadh; he could not weave the heather ropes; he failed to master the principles on which a stalk of corn was erected; and the cart

never went from home without Peggie having
to see that the harness was rightly fixed. It
was only natural that Peggie should come to
have a masterful way about her. And that
masterful way of hers reached its height in
those days which followed that black morning
when Murachadh hanged the cow. It was
their custom to tether the cows of a morning
on the sweet croft grass till breakfast-time, and
one morning, Peggie being taken unwell, the
duty of tethering the animals fell on Murachadh. Now a rope can be tied round an
animal's neck in many ways, and as ill-luck
would have it, Murachadh tied a running noose
on the beasts, and, alas! the noose round the
neck of the best cow slipped. The animal,
feeling the rope tighten, struggled and fell
down a slope, where Murachadh found her
dead, half-suspended by her neck. The loss of
his best cow was to Murachadh the loss of half
his earthly possessions. In face of such a
calamity he could think of nothing but rushing
to the minister. Without a hat, and white

of face, he stumbled into Macleod's presence.

" Oh! she is dead!" cried Murachadh, wringing his hands. " I found her dead."

" Dead," echoed Macleod, well-nigh speechless with the suddenness of the calamity. " When did she get ill? "

" Ill? She wasn't ill at all. I found her dead, hanging by the neck," moaned Murachadh.

" Calm yourself," said Macleod, who felt helpless in face of an experience so rare as suicide. " Whatever has happened she is in the hands of God."

Murachadh looked like a man who, having received a shock so great that he feels he can never receive a greater, yet on the instant receives a greater.

" Mr. Macleod," he said with sudden calmness and dignity, " it is not fitting that you should speak of a cow as if she were a human being and had a soul."

Then the first shock predominated over the second.

"What will Peggie say?" he wailed.

Then Macleod, to his intense relief, realized
that it was the cow, and not Peggie, that was
hung by the neck. When the minister accom-
panied Murachadh to look at the work of his
hands, he found all the animals with running
nooses round their necks. After that morning
Peggie ceased to have a shred of faith in Murachadh so far as the things of this world were
concerned, and from it Dunaluin dated the full
development of Peggie's masterfulness. She
now manifested a desire to make her influence
felt throughout the parish—the croft and the
house being too small a sphere for her admin-
istrative powers.

But even the most managing of women often
have a weakness, and Peggie's weakness was
an idea which possessed her that she had never
quarreled with anyone in her life. When the
neighbors misunderstood her desires to manage
their affairs for them, and resented her actions
in plain terms, Peggie always ended the state-
ment of her wrongs thus: "I cannot under-

stand it, for I never quarreled with anyone in all my life, and never will."

When Macleod brought his young wife to Dunaluin, Peggie was among the first who came to pay their respects. She brought a young fowl with her as an offering wherewith to cement the new friendship. The manse kitchen was spotlessly clean; and the new dish covers freshly polished, shining on the walls, did not find favor in Peggie's eyes. When she returned home, she confided to Murachadh that there was a danger lurking for the minister—the pride of the things of the flesh had entered his dwelling. A year elapsed before Peggie thought it her duty to speak seriously to the minister's wife. She went to the manse with an offering of eggs, and Jean came down to the kitchen with a rose pinned in the bosom of her dress (her husband pinned it there with pretty words that lied not), and a look of wistful happiness lighting up her face, and in her hand a little garment which she was embroidering, and which she had forgotten to lay down. Peggie received her respectfully, and she eyed the little garment, but nothing would stay her purpose. She spoke slowly in that foreign tongue which alone Jean could speak.

"And how is Mr. Macleod?" asked she, when she had said her say about the basket of eggs.

"He is very well," answered Jean. "He is busy to-day at his books and wished not to be disturbed."

"At his books—Eh! but I am pleased at that," resumed Peggie; "for they have been saying that his sermons are not what they were since he married; and I was saying to Murachadh that now he had a wife to speak to and to entertain he would not be studying so much, and that that was why he was falling back in his preaching. The love of the creature is a great snare, as I often say to Murachadh."

A shadow flitted over the fair face of Jean.

Twice after that Peggie went to the manse, and she saw the servant or the minister, but not Jean. When Peggie went home the third time she unburdened herself to Murachadh:

"I cannot understand what has come over the minister's wife. When I used to go to the manse she always came and spoke to me that kindly; but now I have not seen her these three times. One would think I had quarreled with her, but I have never quarreled with anyone all my life and never will, as you know, Murachadh."

Murachadh knew that well; he only grunted and went out to the barn. When Peggie went to see what he was doing she found him praying, kneeling on a heap of clean straw in a corner, and with a look in his face as of a man who was seeing visions of heavenly things. When she saw him at his devotions she left him to his visions, while she returned softly to her work.

One evening, shortly thereafter, Macleod was sitting in his garden. It was early June, and he was enjoying the strange sense of fullness of life which pervades all things, while the earth still retains the freshness of its green. His flowers were springing up around him. He was thinking of the approaching communion season, when the garden gate clicked, and in walked Peggie. When she saw the minister she went straight up to him.

" I was wanting to see you," she said.

" Will we go in or will it do here? " he asked.

" It is better here," she answered, " as what I want to say is for yourself alone. It is about Seonaid I wish to speak. The communion is near, and Seonaid is a member, but she is not in a condition worthy a communicant."

" How is that? " asked the minister. " Remember you are incurring a serious responsibility in making a charge against a member of the Church."

" She wants to quarrel with me," continued Peggie, unabashed; "and anyone who cherishes evil feelings against a neighbor is not fit for the Holy Table."

" What has become between you? " asked Macleod.

"I will tell you that in a moment," resumed Peggie. "You know how much wrapped up Seonaïd is in her children. She cannot bear to punish them; and even on the Sabbath afternoons she lets them out, and they play near the stream that flows beside our croft. Last Sabbath I could hear them laughing as they gathered handfuls of primroses for their mother—it was a fair scandal. I made up my mind to go and speak to her seriously, and on Monday I went. I always make a point of being straightforward and speaking my mind, and I asked her if she had read of the man who was found by the people of God gathering sticks in the wilderness on the Sabbath, and who was brought to Moses and Aaron, and shut up in prison till the will of God was declared regarding him; and how, according to God's will, the whole congregation stoned him with stones outside the camp till he died? Then I told her how her children disturbed the Sabbath peace and gathered flowers. And I reminded her of the words of the wise king,

that he that spareth his rod hateth his son; and drew her attention to his advice, not to withhold correction from the child, for if he be beaten with the rod he shall not die; and how a child left to himself brought his mother to shame. I also gave examples reminding her of the merchant's children, whose mother was so foolish and so fond that she never used the rod on them, and her reward was that they broke her heart. These and other things I said, being a straightforward woman who does not beat about the bush, for I was determined that if these children were lost, it would not be for lack of my doing my simple duty, and being silent when I ought to speak."

Peggie fell silent, having exhausted herself.

"And what did she say to you, Peggie?" asked Macleod.

"Aye, she said enough," began Peggie again. "'How many children have you reared,' says she, 'that you know so much about them?' Then she went to the door and opened it wide.

"'Peggie,' says she in her soft way, 'there's

the way out. I prefer to see the chair you are sitting on empty.' That's what she said, Mr. Macleod.

"I was surprised, for I did not think she would take it that way.

"'Seonaid,' says I, rising and moving towards the door, ' listen to me, and remember that I came here to speak to you for your good. I have never quarreled with anyone in my life, and I am not going to begin with you. God's blessing be with you.'

"But ever since that day Seonaid does not speak to me when we meet. Her conduct is unworthy of a believer. She looks coldly at me, and plainly shows that she has a feeling of anger against me. And it is a defiling of holy things if one comes to the sacrament with ill-feeling in the heart. I thought it my duty to tell you of Seonaid that you may speak to her, and warn her lest she should come to the sacrament in an unworthy condition, and thus incur the great condemnation. I cannot think why Seonaid wants to quarrel with me, for I never quarreled with anyone in my life, and I never will."

When Peggie went away at last, Macleod smiled. It came natural to him to smile in those days.

A SEEKER AFTER TRUTH

A SEEKER AFTER TRUTH

I

THERE was one man in Dunaluin who was a distinct personality by himself. His house was known as the Bighouse, because it was the largest in the parish, and he was always spoken of as if he had been baptized Ardcoran, that being the name of the land which he owned and farmed. He was a man of massive proportions, over six feet high; and year in, year out, he wore the kilt. When he spoke English, which he only did when he was in the company of Dr. Macqueen, or when a stranger came the way, he was easily recognized as an Oxford man. When his father died young Ardcoran came home to look after the paternal land and flocks, and ere he knew it himself, took root there for life. The Bighouse stood on a point of land that jutted westward into the Minch and formed a semicircular bay of white sand. Behind it the land rose gently to the brink of high precipices, in whose caves the rock pigeons nested. The house faced the sun, and from its windows across the isle-studded bay Ardcoran could see the mighty crests of the Coolins, forty miles away. There, night and day, he could hear the wash of the waves, and dream dreams while the voices of the sea lulled all his being to rest. The master of the Bighouse was no mere owner of flocks, he was a man who in his day had cherished ambitions. His ambition had been to publish a book which would go forth from Dunaluin and stir the world. He had got so far as to settle the title; it was to be called " A Search after Truth," but, as he said himself, the climate was too much for him, and there were duties (quoting Carlyle with relish) much more imperative than the writing of books. He was one of the few who went to the parish church and sat under Dr. Macqueen; it was a family tradition to which he strictly adhered. When Ardcoran spoke of going to church, he sometimes declared that he was not quite sure whether he went to church in the ordinary sense of the word, but, at any rate, he attended every Sunday a course of Natural History lectures, which were very instructive, and that was more than could be said of most churches. The only man in the parish with whom Ardcoran was on intimate terms was the Natural History Lecturer, Dr. Macqueen.

The parish looked on Ardcoran as a lost man; for he climbed the hills on Sabbath to have a look at his cattle, and often used language, when he was roused, which would have shamed even our troops when they were in Flanders. But, most of all, the parish trembled for Ardcoran, because he was a professed unbeliever in truths which were clear to Dunaluin—hell was to him a matter for scoffing, and miracles he could not away with. When he discussed these things with Macqueen, he always described himself as a Seeker after Truth. He would fain be a believer; if he could recognize the truth, he would believe it; but, alas! truth was buried in a deep well.

When Dunaluin was stirred to its depths, and the church which used to be thronged was swept away, Ardcoran watched events with an amused and cynical air. Two Sundays after Macleod had passed through the furnace, Ardcoran was missed from the square family pew in Macqueen's church. When they met the minister asked where he had been.

"Since you ask me," answered Ardcoran, "I will tell you honestly. I went to hear the Gospel just for once. This parish of ours cannot endure the Gospel being preached in its simplicity, and they have deserted the man who preached it to the best of his power. I thought to myself I would go and take their place, just for once, to show that there is at least one man in Dunaluin who sets a little store by the teaching of the Man of Peace. You would have been glad I went if you had seen the look of pleasure which came into the face of Macleod when he saw me spreading myself out in the center of the ugly church, trying to fill as much as possible of its emptiness, and you would not have grudged my being away from your lecture."

The old Doctor smiled approvingly at Ardcoran. "I am glad you did that," he said. "It was well done."

"And I am going back again," continued Ardcoran. "You are accustomed to an empty church, but Macleod is not. My going may cheer him a little, and who knows but it may help me in my search. If you miss me, you will know where I am."

"Quite right," said Macqueen with a twinkle in his eye, "you show yourself a better Christian, Ardcoran, than those who think you are none."

"As for them," exclaimed the other, a trifle stung; "they are not Christians at all; they are only fetich-worshipers. When I see people setting up fetiches to worship and fight over I am tempted to throw away the last shreds of religion to which I still cling. Why, you are all fetich-worshipers. At Oxford their form of fetich-worship was candles and millinery (a laughing-stock to men and an offense to angels!); your particular fetich, Macqueen, is what you call the Establishment principles, that, and that alone, you swear by; and these people of Dunaluin have several fetiches—everlasting damnation, original sin, the thrilling delights of the doctrine of election, and many others—which they go forth into the wilderness to worship, breaking the hearts of those who serve them. When I see it all, I say to myself, 'Where is the Lord Jesus Christ that these things are done in His name? He must be powerless and dead.'"

"'A Daniel come to judgment,'" murmured Macqueen, and added aloud, "Aye, the Gospel is truly wounded in the house of its friends."

"Friends! did you say?" asked Ardcoran, "enemies rather! It was when I realized that you were all fetich-worshipers and the enemies of religion that I saw how foolish it was to blame religion for what its enemies did. It is not because of religion, but in spite of it, that these things are done; and I am therefore to keep for a while longer the little of it that I have yet retained, and go on with my Search after Truth."

"And how is the search going on?" queried Macqueen, with his eyes gleaming oddly beneath his shaggy eyebrows.

"Fairly well, fairly well," answered Ardcoran. "I have been reading Spencer lately, and see a ray of light here and there. That last book of the Professor was splendid. He shows that a man can be a Christian without believing in the Incarnation, Resurrection, Miracles, or anything else which is not as clear to him as the fact that two parallel, straight lines can never meet. I was delighted to find that I could claim to be as good a Christian as yourself, Macqueen. You won't mind my giving Macleod a trial now, to see what he can do for me. I'll come round on Mondays to hear any lectures I may miss. That last one I heard on the ' Wisdom of the Creator Manifested in the Wings of the Lepidoptera,' was most instructive."

And Ardcoran whistled to his dog and moved up the road. He courteously returned the salutation of Eachann Donn, who met him; but when the latter stopped as if wishing to speak, Ardcoran walked straight on.

II

THERE was one man in Dunaluin who always spoke well of Ardcoran, and that was
black Hugh, the grieve who managed Ardcoran's home farm. " The best master I ever
had," Hugh would say when he spoke of him.
When anyone remarked in Hugh's hearing
that Ardcoran was a heathen, the reply always
was, " If he is, I wish there were more of his
kind "—(but then only one vote was cast for
Hugh the last time they were electing deacons
in Dunaluin, so that his opinion on questions
of religion could not be said to be prized in the
parish).

Hugh, however, maintained that his master was a good Christian. " Not a night,"
Hugh would assert when he got heated, " but
Ardcoran, ere he goes to sleep, reads a chapter
in his mother's old Bible, and he keeps it on
a shelf to his hand, when he is in bed; that's the

truth, for I have it from a sure hand." Thus would Hugh place his master's position as a religious man beyond dispute.

Hugh was a biased witness, truth to say, for he judged his master's religion by his acts, and in so doing showed how ignorant he was of the vital truths, and how unfit for the office of deacon. For when Hugh's daughter, Effie, was seized with consumption—that scourge of the Hebrides—and the doctor gave it as his opinion that her only chance of life was to go to a dryer climate, it was Ardcoran who sent her southward to seek strength from the sun, and thus added a year or two to her life. And when she returned, and the disease which had been brought for a while to a stand made suddenly another leap forward with doubled strength, reducing Effie to a helpless invalid, it was Ardcoran who brought her delicacies from his own table to tempt her jaded palate, and wine to stem the ebbing of her strength, and with them bright words to cheer her drooping spirit. Little wonder that poor Hugh, to whom Effie was as the apple of his eye, mistook Ardcoran for a good Christian.

There was another who came often to see Effie. Macleod still ministered to the dying as of old, when he was permitted so to do, and poor Effie clung to him. Ever since that day when Macleod laid Dileas in the little church-yard on the hill, there was an added tenderness in his words when he stood by the bedsides of those who were nearing the valley of great shadows. The eyes which suffering had dimmed would light up when Effie saw Macleod come in. The hacking cough ceased to trouble her when she heard him read in her musical, limpid mother-tongue of the shining battlements of the eternal city, of the house not made with hands, of the city whose maker and builder is God, and her eyes would shine as if already the glory of the heavenly places were lighting them.

When the end was near, Effie one day broke in on the reading. "And the city had no need of the sun, neither of the moon, to shine in it——" read the minister very slowly and softly, when, putting her wasted, white hand on his arm, she whispered:

"Tell me, sure, Mr. Macleod, will I go there?"

"I am quite sure you will, Effie," he answered.

"But how are you sure; can I not feel sure too?"

"You may feel quite sure if you trust the Lord Jesus Christ," he answered gently. "Whosoever believeth in Him shall be saved. You believe in Him, and therefore you need not fear. If I said I am coming to-morrow with a gift you would believe me, would you not, because I always do what I promise? And if you would never doubt me, how can you doubt Him who died for you. The Lord will do what He promised. He changeth not. You trust Him, Effie?"

"Yes, I do," she murmured. "I feel at times as if I saw His face in the darkness, smiling upon me."

"Then you may be sure," continued Macleod. "You do your share in the agreement; you trust Him who died for love of you, and liveth to save you; and there is no doubt but He will do His share; bring you to the place where you will see His face. Nothing can pluck you out of His hands."

"Oh, I feel sure now," murmured Effie, "I feel quite sure," and over her face there came the look of one who has come through many perils, and sees the home of her childhood with open door before her.

When Macleod rose from his knees, after the prayer which followed, he discovered that Ardcoran had been kneeling at a chair beside the door. He had come in, unnoticed, while the minister was reading. When the two men had taken leave of Effie, and turned towards the Bighouse, Ardcoran said suddenly:

"For many years I have been a Seeker after Truth; but I have never met anywhere with anything which made it easy to die. I could say nothing to that poor dying girl; I could only give her wine for her body, while her soul was crying for sustenance, hope, and light. But your words made her triumph over her pains and forget her woes. I wish I could believe it as, of course, you do."

To Macleod's ears there seemed to be a query in the words.

"God knows," he replied, "that I have doubted; but I can say truthfully that I now believe with my whole soul that God bringeth life out of death. I cannot explain why I believe; I believe because I feel it is so. Eternal Love cannot be indifferent to the creatures He has made. He did not fashion the fair frame, and create the tender spirit of Effie only to form so much corruption at last. He must have a place elsewhere for her."

"It sounds reasonable," said Ardcoran, "but who knows:

"'Into this universe, and *why* not knowing,
Nor *whence*, like water willy-nilly flowing,
And out of it, as wind along the waste,
I know not *whither*, willy-nilly blowing.'"

Macleod started when he heard old Omar quoted by the shore of the furthest Hebrides.

"We are not a scrap further," continued Ardcoran, "for all our many centuries of boasted knowledge. We know no more than the old Persian."

"You are quite wrong," said Macleod, and he took off his hat. "We have seen the glory of God shining in the face of Jesus Christ; and that glory is Love redeeming from death."

On the following Sunday Ardcoran sat facing Macleod in the desolate church, making something like an oasis in a wilderness of empty pews. The text was the world-old question, "If a man die shall he live again?" The eager look in the face of Ardcoran was almost as inspiring to the preacher as the crowded church used to be. The sermon ended with a quotation:

"For like a child sent with a fluttering light
To feel his way across the gusty night,
Man walks this world. Again and yet again
The lamp shall be by fits of passion slain.

But shall not He, who sent him from the door,
'   Relight the lamp once more, and yet once more ? "

Ardcoran nodded his head; it was a thing he had never done before, but he had to do something to express his surprise at finding some-one else in Dunaluin beside himself who knew something of the Translator of Omàr. " Very neatly quoted," he murmured approvingly, as he walked home with his dog.

III

On that desolate day on which they buried Macleod, it was Ardcoran, standing at the head of the grave, who spoke this eulogy over the dead: "There lieth the best man I ever knew." Later, he spoke his mind to Macqueen on the subject. "Macleod," he declared, "was the truest Christian I ever met. He died, like his Master, serving the people. He had all the 'notes' (that's what you call it in your jargon, Doctor, is it not?) of a Christian. The world hates the true Christian—that's one; it persecutes him—that's two; it reviles him—that's three; it misunderstands him and says he is mad and has a devil—that's four; and if it can, it kills him—that's five. Macleod had all these 'notes.'

"You are all of you doing your best to kill the religion of Jesus Christ," went on Ardcoran, with increasing animation. "Everybody is not like me. I have been a Seeker after Truth, and I can distinguish between religion and its enemies; but the crowd confound religion with those who have the word continually in their mouths, and they cannot see that these men are really the foes of religion. They blame religion for the bitterness and hate and uncharitableness which are making the countryside waste, and the end will be that the rising generation will refuse to have anything to do with it in their disgust. 'If religion is to be forever rousing murderous passions in the hearts of men, we are better without,' they will say. Every chance you get, Doctor, you should point out that all your kind, or most of your kind, are really enemies of the Spirit of God.

"Macleod, almost alone in this place, lived the life of the true Christian; and you saw the end. That man did more than any I ever met to bring me back to the faith in which my mother died. It was not his intellectual power (you have more of that, Doctor), but it was the subtle influence that went forth from a life self-sacrificing and Christlike which well-nigh convinced me that his religion was reality and truth. That man almost brought me to say with Heine at the last: 'I have renounced all philosophic pride, and have returned back to religious ideas and feelings. I die in the belief of one only God, whose pity I implore on my immortal soul.'"

Ardcoran rolled out the quotation with such gusto that Macqueen stroked his gray beard to hide his smile. It was the same Ardcoran still!

"You know the words," continued the Seeker after Truth. "'In every nation he that feareth God and worketh righteousness is accepted with Him.' That is my creed henceforth. With God's help I will be henceforth a worker of righteousness."

And in some measure he was.

Next Sunday Ardcoran was back to his square pew in Macqueen's church, and the Doctor, instead of giving one of his lectures on the plants mentioned in the Bible, preached a sermon, such as he had never preached before, on the words: "Greater love hath no man than this, that a man lay down his life for his friends." At the close of the service Ardcoran, instead of walking straight out whenever the benediction was pronounced, as was his wont, waited behind and shook hands warmly with the old Doctor.

"I apologize," he said, "for my haste in saying that you were one of the enemies of religion, Doctor, and pray your forgiveness."

"There is no need," answered the Doctor cordially; "we know each other too well for that."

"I think," added Ardcoran, "that both you and I, Macqueen, are better men because of him."

Macqueen understood, though no name was mentioned.

"Yes," he answered softly, "he did not serve altogether in vain."

A CHRISTIAN NAME

A CHRISTIAN NAME

It was a great day for Tomas MacGruer when he stood up in the church to get his baby boy baptized. Tomas had had five daughters born to him, and he had despaired of leaving behind him, when he went hence, one who should hand down his euphonious name. But at last, to his great joy, a boy came to him, and Tomas resolved to mark the greatness of the event by calling the child after the minister, just as one of the ancient faith calls a long-prayed-for child after a favorite saint. Murachadh, the beadle, had a specially snow-white napkin that day over the china bowl which did duty for a font; and the minister had a very soft and tender look in his face as he stood on the lowest step of the pulpit stairs and bent over the little burden in Tomas MacGruer's arms. The doors of the church were wide open, and through them those sitting near could see the summer sun flooding the quiet Minch; whiffs of air laden with the perfume of new-mown hay came wafted through the open doors, and a bee could be heard humming in the porch as the congregation held their breath, while the minister sprinkled the water from the china bowl over the white-robed child and uttered the sacred words, " William Macleod, I baptize thee in the name of the Father, and of the Son, and of the Holy Ghost. Amen." Ann, the proud mother, wept softly in a corner of the nearest pew, and the face of Tomas showed a mingled feeling of pride and discomfort, of joy and dismal helplessness such as most men feel on similar occasions. After the service a crowd of women thronged round and paid homage to young William Macleod MacGruer —a homage which he received with the stolidity of a Buddhist idol. For the rest of that day Tomas MacGruer was the happiest man in Dunaluin.

If the son had been born to Tomas MacGruer

six months later, he would not have received
the name he did; for Tomas felt very sore over
the minister's having denied the faith, as they
said in Dunaluin, and having elected to continue
minister of a church which was not according
to the people's standard of what a pure church
should be. Tomas went with the rest who
thronged the quarry, having left Macleod like
a voice crying in a wilderness of rotting pews.
The child's name was the fly in the ointment of
Tomas' happiness in those days.

One evening, when Tomas had gone out
with the nets, and Ann was at home spinning
by the fire, and the child in the cradle beside
her cooing to his toes, two of the good women
of Dunaluin walked in—Seonag, the wife of
Eachann Donn, and Ishabel, who was not the
wife of any man, but who was reputed the most
religious and zealous woman in all the countryside. When the visitors had sat in to the fire,
'Ann laid aside her wheel, and lifted the baby to
show his charms. She pointed out his dimples,
the little sharp teeth beginning to peep here and

there through the red gums, and the curls
round his forehead; but the two women were
strangely silent. They looked at the child with
pitying eyes and said nothing.

" He is a nice boy," said Seonag at last, " but
what a misfortune it is that he should bear
the name of a man who has fallen away from
grace."

" Och! Och! " moaned Ishabel, " a misfortune indeed! "

" I would not have any son of mine bear his
name," went on Seonag, warming to her subject. " Did you ever hear how Eachann found
him out? "

" Tell us, Seonag," said Ishabel, who knew
only too well.

" It was one day when he was preaching, a
year ago," went on Seonag. " His subject was
the storm on the lake, when the Lord came
walking on the sea to His disciples. He
described the whole thing—the waves breaking
white in the night; the dark clouds hiding the
moon and the stars, and the frightened men at

the oars—till you felt as if you almost saw it.
It was a murky night, so dark that the Lord
walking over the sea did not see the boat.
Suddenly a rift came in the storm-driven clouds
and the moon shone out on the trembling water,
and then the Lord saw the disciples, with the
fear of death in their eyes, toiling at rowing.
Just think of it" (and Seonag lowered her
voice to an awesome whisper), "the Lord who
saw all things, for whom the night shineth as
the day, could not see the danger of His disciples till the moon shone out."

"Och! Och!" moaned Ishabel, "an unbeliever, sure enough!"

"Eachann distrusted him more than ever
from that day," continued Seonag; "and everybody sees now that Eachann was right."

"But he is a kind man and has a good heart,"
said poor Ann feebly, holding her boy tightly
to her breast.

"What is the good of being a kind man?
Domhnull Cam is a kind man, but everybody
knows what he is, for all that. What is the

good of being kind when he does not believe the Bible is true from beginning to end; when he stayed in a Church which allows ministers to teach there was no such person as Adam—only worms or monkeys; when he does not believe in even the fire of hell, for I heard him with my own ears say that the worst pain was not what the body was called on to endure, but what the spirit endured, and that thus hell was not bodily, but spiritual pain. ' Aye,' says I, ' what is the good of his being kind when he has proved a traitor to the truth, and has shown himself in his true character as a false prophet?' "

" Och! Och! " moaned Ishabel, rocking herself backward and forward. " A false prophet he is indeed. I could cry when I see the poor innocent who is doomed to bear his name."

Beyond the hallan there came a cackle and a flap of wings. A fowl, which had strayed, was seeking her place for the night on the spars.

" It was not our fault," said Ann, beginning

to cry over the disgraced baby who was now
sleeping in her bosom. "We all thought so
much of him at that time."

"So we did," replied Seonag; "all except
Eachann, whose eyes God opened to recognize
the danger lurking for the parish; and all our
eyes are opened now. No child should bear
the name of a man who has sold his heritage in
the Church of God for a mess of pottage, and
has gone astray to walk in the ways of Jero-
boam, the son of Nebat, who made Israel to
sin."

"Och! Och!" moaned Ishabel, rocking from
side to side and wiping her eyes. "He has
become a worshiper of idols, setting more value
on the opinions of men than on the word which
cannot lie."

Another belated fowl cackled beyond the
hallan and fluttered up to the spars.

"It cannot be helped now," said Ann, weep-
ing bitterly.

"But it can," said Seonag, coming to the
point. "The registrar can stroke out the name

and put another in its place if you send Tomas
to speak to him.   It is easily done, and I would
do anything, if I were you, to save the child
from bearing such a name."

Ann began to dry her eyes.

"When Tomas comes home I will speak to
him about it," she said.

Seonag and Ishabel went out into the fast
falling night, feeling that they had done their
duty by Ann and her boy.   They congratulated
each other as they made their way homeward
over the stubble.

II

THAT same night a tap came to the door of the schoolhouse on the moor where Mr. Padruig sat up late, mending a watch. He was a man who discharged many offices. His paid duties were those of schoolmaster, poor-law office, and registrar; but in addition to these he discharged many other duties, as watchmaker, apothecary, and veterinary surgeon through all the wide parish. His favorite hobby was to clean and mend watches, and the man who gave him a watch to mend conferred a favor on him. He was studying the flywheel of an errant watch that night when the knock came to the door, and in response to his hearty "Come in," Tomas walked into the room. As he took a chair, Padruig noticed that he looked abashed and uncomfortable, very different from his usual self-satisfied manner. He sat a long while before he came to the point.

"Anything wrong with your watch?" said Mr. Padruig at last.

"No, she is all right, master."

"The cow, perhaps?"

"No, she is all right."

"Quite well yourself?"

"Yes, all right."

"What can I do for you, then?" asked Padruig, with patience outworn.

"It is Ann who sent me," said Tomas, Adamlike; "and she sent me to see if I could get the name of the boy changed. She wants to change the name and call the boy Eachann."

Padruig allowed the watch-glass which he held in his hand to fall in his astonishment. It was not a cow or a horse or a disordered human stomach this time!

"Why do you want it changed?" he asked, feeling that he was within sight of something interesting.

"I will tell you that, master," replied Tomas, feeling more comfortable now that the ice was broken. "When I was out on the sea to-day

Seonag and Ishabel came to see my wife and talked to her of the disgrace it was to have the boy bearing the name of a man who proved unfaithful to the good cause, and they told her you could change the name in the books. If you could do it for us, it would be a great favor, master."

" Do you wish it changed, yourself? " asked Padruig, looking steadily at him.

" Yes, I do," answered Tomas. " I do not wish the boy to continue bearing the name of a man who has stayed in a Church which has betrayed her trust. I would like the name changed."

" Do you remember when you were very ill, two years ago, how good Mr. Macleod was to you, Tomas? "

" I remember that he was very kind, but what of that? "

" Do you remember when your little girl was near death, as we all thought, how he used to come and lift her in his arms and tell her of the Good Shepherd; and do you remember how she would be quiet with him when she would bear no one else?"

"Yes, I remember; but anyone would do that. It was only kindness."

"Do you remember two years ago after you were ill, when Dr. Macqueen gave you meal, and you were ashamed to go to him again, how you went to Mr. Macleod, and he gave you money to pay your way south, which you have not, perhaps, paid him back yet?"

Tomas winced at that.

"It was so," he said. "He was always kind; I will say that of him."

"And you yet wish the name changed?"

"Yes, I do," Tomas replied doggedly. "What is the good of a man being kind when he is unsound in the vital principles of the faith?"

Padruig had a sharp tongue, when he was roused, and he now stood up, crunching under his feet the bits of broken glass on the stone floor.

"Look here, Tomas," he said with his eyes

gleaming; "your surname, MacGruer, is about the ugliest I have ever come across in my life, and the people who bear it are of rather a low breed—needy, improvident, seekers after charity, and ungrateful withal. It would give me pleasure to help the boy to get rid of that name. Any other name, say M'Cruslick, M'Talla, or M'Kien, would be an improvement on MacGruer. We can easily manage that. But not even the Queen or the Parliament can change the name which a man gets when he is baptized, for it is by the ordinance of the unchangeable God that the name is given."

Padruig produced a key and opened his safe. Out of it he took a big ledger which Tomas had seen six times in his life.

"Since you spoke of changing names," went on Padruig, "I may as well change MacGruer and put down M'Kien or M'Codrum. I am sure the boy will be grateful, when he grows up, to be saved from answering to a name which is only borne by mean men, and a name which is the ugliest in the Island. Which name will I change it to?"

"You will not change it at all," said Tomas stiffly. "The name was good enough for my father and for me, and it is good enough for the boy."

"Then, Tomas," said Padruig, and his words cut like lances, "you can be going home. I have seen a good many men making fools of themselves in my life, but I have never seen a man making a greater fool of himself than you have done at the bidding of two old women."

And Padruig opened the door, through which Tomas went out, crestfallen, into the darkness.

When Padruig picked up the pieces of broken glass the hard look faded out of his face little by little, till at last he laughed heartily.

"I must tell this to the Doctor," he said to himself; "he will enjoy it."

But Macqueen felt far from enjoying it, when he heard the story.

'A MARRIAGE WITHOUT 'A WOOING

A MARRIAGE WITHOUT A WOOING

Towards the end of a week in the early spring a rumor went through the parish that Colin, the son of Domhnull Ban, who lived beside the church at Balmeanach, was to be married at last, and that the proclamation was to be made on Sunday. The news created the greatest interest; for everybody was much interested in Colin's forthcoming marriage, and the interest was intensified by the fact that, though it was well known that Colin meant to get married, none knew who was to be the bride, and some went so far to say that even Colin himself did not know. Nobody in all the district was so much interested as the old parish minister, for Colin was one of the very few who worshiped in his church; and, besides, Colin was his nearest neighbor.

Every time Macqueen looked out of his

window he saw Colin's house, with its gable-
end towards the road, and a green hillock
before its door, and beyond it the deep-blue,
shimmering sea. The minister was fond of
looking from his window at the wide expanse
of weltering waves that filled the Minch—the
ever-varying pictures he saw reflected there as
in a mirror were his only companions; and
ever in the foreground he saw Colin's house;
and often on the green hillock before his door
he would see Colin himself, standing like a
statue looking westward to where the heavens,
bending low, touch the hills of Barra, making
in the sunset an arc of glory overhanging a sea
of gold. Whenever the minister looked westward in the evening and saw Colin on his
hillock, with his eyes also fixed on the emerald
sky and shining sea, he felt a touch of sympathy for Colin; doubtless he also was a lover
of the sea.

To the minister Colin's house was a source
of continual wonder. The first time he visited
it—it was forty years ago, and he was young

then and fresh from the Divinity Hall of a
great city—he felt that the centuries were
blotted out, and that he was back among the
primitive ages.   Its low, thick walls were built
of rough, unhewn stones, that were held together with earth and clay—there was no trace
of lime.   The roof was of thatch, which was
kept in its place by heather ropes weighted with
heavy stones, that hung over the walls, forming
a girdle round the house.   Though many years
had passed since Macqueen first saw it, the
house was still the same.   The first room as
one entered at the door near the gable was
Colin's hospital for his cattle.   There he kept
any cow or calf that required special attention;
and the hospital, truth to tell, was never without a patient.   A rough wooden partition
separated this room from the kitchen; and the
door between had no lock, but by pulling a
string that peeped out through a hole, the
visitor could lift the wooden latch and gain
entrance.   In the center of the earthen floor,
on a hearth built of rough stones raised slightly

above the floor-level, the peat-fire always glowed brightly; and, there being no chimney, the smoke hung heavy overhead and filled all the room, its only outlet being a barrel out of which the bottom had been knocked, fixed in the thatch overhead. One pane of glass set in the thatched roof admitted all the light that was required. From a rafter above the fire hung a chain black and thick-crusted with the soot of many years, and by it the three-legged pots were suspended over the fire. In a third room, which was entered from the kitchen, were two wooden beds and a table. This was the superior room of the house, for it had a four-paned window, fixed, not in the thatch, but in the rough wall.

More than a year had passed since Colin's father, Domhnull Ban, lay dying in this inner room. He had lived in the same house all his days, and he was now over ninety years of age. When asked how old he was, the old patriarch answered: "The days of the years of my pilgrimage are fourscore and twelve

years; few and evil have the days of the years
of my life been, and have not attained unto
the days of the years of the life of my fathers
in the days of their pilgrimage." The reek
always lay heavy in the four corners of the
room and hung like a dark cloud overhead, and
from beyond the hallan there usually came the
sound of a cow softly chewing her cud—a
soothing, restful sound, suggestive of clover-
fields and summer days; and the minister often
thought, when he visited the dying man to read
to him the words of eternal consolation by the
light of the glowing peat-fire, that he was never
in a more solemn place.

This house of Colin is not a thing of the
past; strange to say, in this age of progress,
it still stands unchanged, and many such can
yet be found in the lonely Hebrides, where
the lives of the people are untouched by the
march of that civilization which leaves white-
walled cottages in its wake. In it Colin's
father lived for over ninety years, and Colin
hopes to equal the number of his father's days.

For, if the house be rough and bare and un-
adorned, is not the grandeur of nature all
around it? Does not the great sea sing hour
by hour to the shore? The air is soft and clear,
and the perfume of the thyme is in it; the
green grass grows all around; the murmur of
running water is near, and the hillsides are
flecked with heather. A poor, miserable house;
but, remembering the horrors of one-roomed
houses down in the slums, we think that Colin,
sitting by his bright peat-fire, is in an enviable
position, even though the peat-reek hangs in
clouds around him.

After Domhnull Ban's death the daughter
that so long had cared for him married, and
Colin was left alone to manage the croft and
cattle. For a few months he struggled on
bravely; but things went from bad to worse.
As the spring advanced it looked as if Colin
would soon have all his cattle under his own
roof, for one by one he was bringing them in
to his hospital.

The house had to be approached with cau-

tion; and one evening, when the minister went
to see him, Colin began to tell his troubles.
The spring work was beginning.   He had none
to work after the crooked spade and put the
potato-seed in the furrow.   "I will tell you
what it is, minister," he exclaimed.   "I am
like Murachadh Og when he lost his gray mare.
You know what Murachadh said when he
looked at the carcass of the mare?"

"No," said Macqueen, "I never heard."

"What! never heard that?" said Colin,
"When Murachadh looked long at the dead
mare he cried, 'Och! och!   There is no help
for it now, but I must get a wife.'   I am like
him, minister; I must get a wife."

Now, Colin was at least fifty years of age.
He was big in stature, rugged in face, with
straggling beard and scanty hair—loose-jointed
and shambling in gait.   He always wore homespun and a blue Kilmarnock bonnet.   Not even
his mother could say that his appearance was
in any way captivating.

The minister, though he encouraged Colin,

thought that perhaps he would not get a wife so easily as he fancied; and so it turned out. Colin did not lack zeal in his quest; but the quest after a while seemed doomed to failure. For this the minister was sorry; though Colin was uncouth, yet he had watched tenderly over his old father, and he had a good, kind heart. So, when the news came that the wife had been found at last, the minister looked forward to his interview with Colin with much interest; and when, late on Saturday night, he heard voices at the manse door, he knew it must be Colin; and Colin it was. Holding his blue bonnet in his hand, and looking like a man who had been through much trouble and had not known sleep for many nights, rather than an expectant bridegroom, he was ushered into the minister's study. Then, without uttering a word, he sat and gazed moodily at the fire. It was only when the minister at last said, " I am glad to hear that you are getting married," that Colin found his voice.

" Getting married, am I? " he said. " If I

am, it is myself who am the miserable man.
Listen to me, and I will tell you all about it.
You remember, minister," he said, " advising
me to get a wife. I tried to follow that advice;
but I did not find it easy. Last week, however,
Seumas Ruadh, the merchant over in Minginish, sent me word that he had a wife ready
for me. It is myself who was glad when I
heard it; and on Tuesday I put the cows in
early and fed them, and smoored the fire.
Then, as the shadows were creeping on, in the
mouth of the night [*ann am bheul na h'oidche*]
I set out for my eighteen miles' tramp to Minginish. Soon it got very dark, and the cries
of the sea-birds died down; and as I walked
through the black darkness I could hear nothing but the wash of the waves on the pebbly
shore. When I was passing the inn at Dunskiath I thought I would get a bottle of the
good *uisge-beatha,* so in I went. ' Give me,'
said I, ' a bottle of your real Talisker. I am
going to a *reiteach* ' [betrothal], said I; ' and
if you give me any of the poison you give the

'drovers I'll pay you out.'   You know the stuff, minister?"

"Yes; the whisky that makes a man feel, when he has taken a glass, as if a torchlight procession had gone down his throat," said the minister.

"Never heard of that kind of light," said Colin; "but the innkeeper disappeared, and he soon came back with a black and dusty bottle, and he said I would have to pay six shillings for it.   Six shillings for a bottle of *uisge-beatha!* Who ever heard of such a price?   I gave him five; and, stuffing the bottle into my pocket, I struck out again for Minginish.

"It was eleven o'clock when I got to Seumas Ruadh's house; and Seumas was gone to bed, and his wife said I could not see him till morning.   'Go you up to him,' said I, 'and tell him that the man from Dunaluin, for whom he has got a wife, is here; and tell him that if he is not down here immediately I'll come up where he is, and we will see what will happen then.' So up she went; and in about five minutes down he came buttoning his coat, and he said he was glad to see me. He sent a messenger to the house of the woman he had found for me, and in a little while Seumas and I stepped out into the night; and about twelve o'clock we came to her house.

" Sitting at a bright fire we found a pleasant-faced old man and woman, and they bade us welcome, saying it was a cold night, and inviting us to sit close to the fire. ' It is raw and cold indeed,' I said; 'but I have a drop of the real Talisker, and you will not think me forward if I offer a taste all round?' They said they seldom tasted the good liquor, but out of courtesy they would take some from me, and that all the more readily because they knew my father—the good old man, who had gone home —peace be with him! So I gave them all a taste of the good liquor, and I took some myself. Dhe! but that *uisge-beatha* was good, if it was dear. It went down to my toes and up to my hair; it ran through my veins and loosened my tongue; and when we looked at each other after drinking it we seemed one to the other to be much younger, and in the eyes of the old man and woman there came a look of other days.

" Then Seumas Ruadh began to speak. He told them what a decent man I was; how my father died, and my sister married, and I was left alone with three cows and a croft, and how much I needed a wife. After he had said all the good he could imagine about me, he then said that I had heard what a good, dutiful daughter Mairi was, and that I had come in the hope that they would give her to me for wife.

" So there," exclaimed Colin, " was that darned merchant (begging your pardon, minister) asking their daughter for me as my wife, and I had never seen her in my life. They said they were both agreeable, knowing that I was a decent man; but that I had better ask Mairi herself. In a little Mairi came in, and when she did—well, when I saw her wasn't I sorry that I had left Dunaluin in the mouth of the night, and didn't I wish myself back again!"

"Why, what was wrong with her?" asked the minister.

"Oh, she was that black," said Colin. "Her hair was like the soot on the barrel on the top of my house, and her skin as brown as that of a Hindu. Now, I always liked a fair skin and yellow hair," continued the sentimental Colin; "but, ach! she was that black."

"Black, but comely," put in the minister.

"Comely! Nothing of the kind. She had hardly a nose to speak of; and her face was marked—I am sure she has had the smallpox—black and pock-marked!"

"Was that all?" asked the minister.

"Not nearly all!" exclaimed Colin. "She was short and plump, and had no waist—just like a sack of wool with a string tied round the middle."

"Surely you saw something nice about her, Colin," said the minister.

At this Colin looked into the fire and thought

a little. "Well," he resumed after a pause,
"yes, she had nice brown eyes, and she looked
kind when she smiled. But when I saw her it
was myself who was the miserable man. What
was I to do? I felt that I didn't care whether
she accepted me or not, so I asked her straight,
'What Church are you of?' 'Free Church,'
says she. 'Well, I am a Moderate myself,'
says I, 'and you will have to come to the
Moderate Church with me if you marry me.'
'But my conscience won't allow me to do that,'
says she. 'Your conscience?' says I. 'If it
is your conscience you are to obey and not your
husband, then I will be bidding you good-night,
and going back to Dunaluin just as I came.'
'But there is no life in your Church,' says she.
'No life in our Church—isn't there?' I replied. 'What life is there in yours? I am
hearing that your professors have proved that
all our life has come to us through gorillas and
monkeys from the sand-worms that are on the
shore below my croft; and if that be the life in
your Church, you are welcome to it.' And so

I put on my bonnet to start for home, full of rage," concluded Colin.

"That was a queer way to woo a wife, Colin," said Macqueen.

"Queer! Well, so it was; but it was as good as any other. For she no sooner saw how determined I was than she said that wherever I went she would go. At this I sat down, and we had another taste of the good and generous *uisge-beatha*. When I had taken another mouthful of it, oh! I declare to you, minister, Mairi looked beautiful and young in my eyes. Strange thing the *uisge-beatha!* And the old man, warmed by it, became generous, and he said he would give Mairi his best cow, and the old woman said she had a trunk full of blankets and clothes for Mairi; and ere I knew where I was or how it happened I found myself on the way home in the gray dawn of morning, having agreed to marry Mairi first week. She is to be proclaimed to-morrow in the church at Minginish; and, oh, minister! I have changed my mind. I cannot go on with it; she is that black. It is myself who am the miserable man."

"She is to be proclaimed to-morrow at Minginish, you say?" asked the minister; "and are you not to be proclaimed here and go on with it?"

"*Donus mir!* not if I can help it," said Colin.

"Then that will be very dishonorable," exclaimed the minister.

"It is all very well for you, minister," said Colin; "but you have not seen her, and I have; and it is not you who are to marry her, but me."

"Well, Colin," answered the minister, "if you do not go on as you promised, I will tell you what will happen. You will be summoned before the sheriff for disgracing that woman in Minginish. You will have made her the talk of the Island, and the end of it will be she will get some twenty pounds damages off you."

At this he gasped.

"Do you really mean it?" was his anxious query.

"Yes, certainly," said the minister; "and you will have richly deserved it."

Then there was a long pause, and at last Colin said, "What must be, must be. You will proclaim us to-morrow, minister, and marry us on Thursday."

So it was arranged. Colin rose heavily and passed slowly out; and as he descended the stairs the minister thought he heard him mutter, "Twenty pounds if I don't marry her, and she is that black! *Mo truaigh mise!* It is myself who am the miserable man."

On Thursday the minister married them; but that is another story. On Sunday, Colin and Mairi came to be kirked, and Mairi sat very close to Colin—perhaps she felt a little afraid, never having been in a Moderate church before; and Colin looked as proud and happy as if he had been a bridegroom of thirty who had wedded and won the love of his youth after much waiting.

. . . . . .

After four years Macqueen was paying one

of his infrequent visits (he was of the old
school, and did not believe in much visiting),
and he found Colin standing on the green hillock as of yore, facing the great sea, where the
lights and shadows came and went. He was
no longer alone, for he had with him a smart
little boy dressed in a tartan kilt, who ran after
the cows and the fowls. The minister soon
found that it was useless to talk to Colin about
anything but the boy.

"Look at him, now," exclaimed Colin; " did
you ever see a boy two years old quicker than
that boy? Isn't he a wise one, now? He
knows the cows by name and runs after them
from morn to eve. I tell you, minister, I never
knew the Gaelic was such a sweet language
till I heard that little chap call me *pada;* it was
like the song of larks and the ripple of our
brook rolled into one. There is only one thing
that troubles me now, and that is the thought
that in all probability I cannot live to see that
little man grown up. I wish I had married
years ago." Then pointing with his hand to

the house, where the reek ascended as of old through the barrel that had no bottom, he said, "Minister, that little man's mother is the best wife in all Dunaluin. She is all white and golden—she is. Lucky the day it was for me when I married her, though I had never so much as seen her when Seumas Ruadh in Minginish asked her for me from her father. That was a good turn Seumas did for me. The old house, with wife and bairn in it, is very different from the place as it was when I was alone and you used to come and see me."

When the minister saw Mairi and spoke to her of Colin, she answered with shining eyes, "It is the good and kind husband that Colin is to me, minister; never a better in all Dunaluin."

THE WANDERER'S RETURN

THE WANDERER'S RETURN

I

NEAR the manse in which the old parish
minister had lived for well-nigh two generations there lived an aged widow, Mary Mac-
Raild, or Mairi Bhan, as she was known to her
neighbors. Her house was about the best of
its kind in the parish, for it had windows set
in the wall, and two chimneys, while the thatch
was kept in its place, not by heather ropes, but
by wire netting. That was in itself a mark of
distinction! She lived alone, for her family
were all grown up and settled in homes of
their own, some in the parish and some far
away.

There was one son who of all her children
was the most mindful of his mother, and it was
of him that she loved to speak. She lacked for
nothing, she used to say to her neighbors; for

had she not always kept her cow? and was not the minister kind in giving her potato-ground on his glebe? and did not Alastair, who digged for gold in far-off Queensland, always remember her?

Her red-letter days were those in which Alastair's letters came. She could not read, but by the color of the stamp she knew her son's letter. Holding it in her lap, she would sit for a while pondering by the fire. Then she always dressed herself carefully, put on her best black dress, a snow-white mutch, and the Paisley shawl, which she only produced on great occasions; and, with her letter hid securely in her breast, she would go round and ask for the minister. Nobody else was deemed worthy of the great trust of opening these precious letters.

Carefully did Macqueen open these letters. It was a point of honor with them that the letter should be read first ere the little thin paper, which in some strange way could be turned into money, was looked at. The letters, truth to tell, were always pretty much the same; for Alastair did not excel with his pen. The great item of news was always put first—he was well. (At this there would come a sigh of relief from the gentle face that looked wistfully at the minister from below the mutch). The weather was very hot, and the land was parched for want of rain.

"Is that not strange, now?" Mairi would say, "for we have had nothing but rain these many months."

"But this is from the other side of the world," the minister would answer; while Mairi strove in vain to imagine a world different from that Isle which was all the world she knew.

Then the letter would be resumed.

Food was very dear, and this prevented his saving money very fast. Butter was four shillings the pound, and eggs five shillings the dozen.

"Five shillings the dozen, did you say, minister?" Mairi would exclaim, "and I sell mine for sixpence to Calum Ruadh, the merchant. Oh! they are robbing poor Alastair."

But Macqueen would go on with the letter, which always concluded by telling Mairi not to be saving the money that was inclosed, but to spend it on her needs and to be good to herself; for he was coming home soon, and, unless his mother was provided with everything she required, then he would be very angry.

And Mairi would wipe the tears from her eyes.

It was only then that the minister unfolded the blue paper.

"It is £10 this time, Mairi. What do you wish done with it?"

"You will be good enough to send it to the bank at Port-a-Righ," she always answered. "What a good son he has been to me! The others always had enough to do to provide for themselves, but he never forgot his mother. And you will get the money put in his name and my own—will you not?"

"Will you not keep some?" Macqueen

always asked; "and will it not do to have the receipt in your own name alone?"

"I do not need any," was the unfailing answer, "for Alastair put money in the bank the last time he came home, and he arranged that the interest should be always sent to me. That is enough for my needs."

Thus it was that each half-year, when Alastair's letter came, the money went to the bank at Port-a-Righ, and was placed there in the joint-names of mother and son.

"You see," she said, "if I do not live until he comes back, he will find it all safe there; and he will know that his mother was thinking of him."

And as the half-years passed, and each letter said that he was coming soon, the yearning in her heart grew greater that Alastair might come back, and that she might see his face ere she died.

But the lines were deepening on her face, and the look of wistfulness was becoming more constant in her eyes. The neighbors, to whom she often spake of how Alastair was coming soon, would say, as they watched her steps growing feebler, that, unless he came very soon, poor Mairi Bhan would never see her son again.

II

THE great event of the year in the parish of Dunaluin is the Communion. It is the point from which they reckon the history of the months. If one is asked when such and such a thing occurred, the answer is so many weeks before or after the Communion. They always hold it during the fairest month of the year—in June. There is then a lull in the onward progress of the weeks. The plots of ground are tilled and sown and green with the growing crops; the peats are cut, and drying, heaped up, in the summer sun; and the men are not yet gone to the fishing. In this time of leisure from the world's labor the thoughts of all the people are turned to the most solemn rite of their faith. For five days the services go on, and while they last no work is done. The number of worshipers is so great—for they

gather from all the neighboring parishes—that
the services are held in the open air. The spot
selected for these conventicles is wonderfully
beautiful. It is a hollow beside the sea, where
the minister's tent is erected with its back to
the shore, and the people are massed on the
semicircular rising ground in front, facing the
tent and the shimmering water beyond. One
can see no more solemn sight in all the Isles
than these great Communion services. The
lapping of the waves mingles with the wail of
the psalms, chanted by some two thousand
people, on whom the sun pours down its light
from a clear sky like a blessing from God. He
who sees it for the first time cannot but think of
Him who preached to the multitudes on the
shores of Gennesaret, with the ripple of the
waves on the strand as the undertone of the
words of life that fell from His lips. Before
the tent extends the white-covered table at
which the communicants sit; and the most
solemn moment of all is when the aged men
and women rise, while the psalm is being sung,

and make their way slowly and with faltering steps to their Lord's Table set for them in the wilderness. Sometimes the psalm has to be sung twice ere all muster up courage to take their place, so sacred and so solemn is the great ordinance to those dwellers in the mist. In all the great assembly not more than thirty venture to go forward to the table; for all the rest it is not a Communion in the real sense, only the most awesome spectacle of the year.

This year old Mairi became more wistful and tender as the great season came round. She had not yet mustered up courage to ask to be admitted to the Communion, though she had often longed to partake; but she now felt her day was nearly done, and that, if she was to confess her Lord before men, she must not let another opportunity pass; and accordingly she, with many misgivings, appeared before the Session, who were to judge of her fitness for the sacred ordinance.

It happened that there was no minister then in Dunaluin, but one was sent to dispense the

Sacrament, and before him and the elders Mairi appeared. She was the only one who did so, so few were they who deemed themselves worthy to partake. When she went into the room where the meeting was held, she explained with quavering voice that, as she was unable to read, she could not learn or say her Catechism.

"You know," said Eachann Donn, who was the spokesman of his fellow-elders, "that our rule is that the communicants must know their Catechism. Now tell us, what is God?"

"God is love; God is my Father," she answered.

"But that is not the answer in the Catechism, and that is what we want," said Eachann. "What is justification by faith?"

"I know only," she answered, "that I trust wholly in the Lord Jesus, and that I love Him."

The minister looked troubled; but he was not a strong man, and, being a stranger, he was loath to interfere with the men who managed the congregation. So Eachann went on with his questions, and Mairi answered in her own way, but not according to the book.

After a little the minister and elders conferred apart; and then the minister said very gently that, for his part, he was very willing to admit Mairi to the Communion; but that the elders deemed it best she should wait another year and get someone to teach her the Catechism, and then they would admit her.

"But I may not live to see another year," she answered through her tears.

"That is in God's hand," said Eachann; "and we cannot admit you unless you know as much as we require of all our communicants."

Then she rose to go out. At the door she turned and said: "Eachann Donn, you can shut me out from the Communion; but, thank God, you cannot shut me out of heaven."

The day was one of the few hot days which are seen in the Hebrides. The midsummer sun poured down its rays from a clear sky. There was no wind, and the sea that stretched out from the side of the road that led to Mairi's house was motionless as glass. A mile out a large steamer was passing up the Minch, and the black mass of smoke from its funnel was the only shadow on the face of the deep. She had two miles to walk in the pitiless heat, and she was already wearied with the way she had come. The excitement had exhausted her. The feeling that she was now disgraced before all the parish seemed to choke her. Her brain throbbed with racking pain. Her one thought was to hurry home and hide herself. The road looked to her as if it were heaving in billows before her. She staggered, but recovered herself; then again she faltered, and fell senseless at the roadside. There a passing neighbor found her, and brought her home in his cart. Her family gathered round her, and gently they laid her on her bed. Two days she lingered, but she was unable to speak. Twice did the old minister, her neighbor, read and pray with her, and her eyes watched him intently. The last time he read to her the wondrous vision of John, who saw the new

Jerusalem and the followers of the Lamb. "'They shall hunger no more, neither thirst any more,'" he read very slowly. . . "'And God shall wipe away all tears from their eyes.'" When he stopped, she tried to speak. Her son declared that the words she tried to utter were, "He will not shut me out." Ere the prayer which followed was finished Mairi Bhan had gone to Him who said, "Him that cometh to Me, I will in no wise cast out."

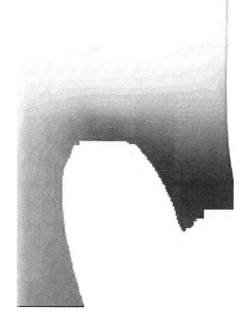

III

Two months after Mairi Bhan was laid to
her rest, there landed from the steamer at
Dunskiath a bronzed and stalwart passenger.
There was nobody to meet him, for nobody expected him; and among the little company that
waited the steamer's coming there was none
who knew him. He made his way to the inn,
and, hiring a dogcart, drove off without delay
to Dunaluin. Alastair MacRaild had come
home from the far-off gold fields of Australia,
and in his eyes there was a light which is only
to be seen in the eyes of those who return after
long years to the mothers they love. As he
drove rapidly through the heather-covered
moors, and felt the sweet air with the perfume of the thyme brushing his face, he drew
long breaths. It was good to be alive, he felt.
As the evening shadows were lengthening, at a

sudden turn of the road he saw the long coast-
line of Dunaluin stretching forth before him in
reaches of sand diversified by rocks, tapering
to a point in the Aird, which stretched far out
into the sea, pointing to the west. The line
where the shore and the sea met was drawn in
loops and curves; and all the little bays and
havens, where the waves danced gently, had
each for him a memory of other days. From
all the houses that were dotted over the slopes
the smoke rose in straight columns, and then
spread out fanlike over the land, for the evening was very still. The wanderer felt a lump
rising in his throat as he feasted his eyes on it
all. In all the world there was not such a
peaceful scene as this—the home of his youth,
which he meant to leave no more. The night
was falling rapidly, and in the gathering gloom
he met none who knew him. As he wished to
come quietly to his mother, he told the driver
to turn a mile from her house, and that last
mile he walked rapidly with fast-beating heart.
With trembling hand he opened the wicket-

gate, set in the bourtree hedge he knew so well.
There was no light in the house. He tried to
open the door, but it would not give. He
turned to the window, and he saw that it was
covered with dust. At the sight a great fear
seized him. Over the place he felt the brood-
ing silence which one only feels in a deserted
house.

The nearest house was the manse, and thither
he ran. It was a white, drawn face that the
servant saw when she opened to him, and it
was a strained voice she heard asking for the
minister. The old man was at home; and
when he saw the long-yearned-for son enter
his room with a look of agony on his face, a
feeling of great pity seized him, and he could
find no words. It was in silence that the two
men clasped hands.

"My mother!" said Alastair brokenly, as
he took the proffered chair by the peat fire that
glowed in the grate. "Where is she?"

"Oh, Alastair!" answered Macqueen,
"have you not heard? It is sorry I am to be

the first to tell you the sore news. Your
mother is gone to her rest."

And Alastair buried his face in his hands;
but through his fingers the minister saw the
salt tears falling. For a long while there was
silence in the room, broken only by the half-
smothered sobs of a man who half-an-hour ago
was the strongest of the strong. Then, when
he was master of himself again, Alastair raised
his head and looked at the minister.

" Tell me about her death," he said.

Very gently and slowly the old minister told
him all, deeming it better that he should hear it
from him than that he should be left to gather
the garbled stories of the people. Slowly and
reluctantly he told it, for he knew the pain it
would cause him. When the sad story was
ended there was again a long silence, while the
peats were moldering into gray ashes before
them.

" Oh! how could they treat my mother so? "
Alastair at last exclaimed. " She was the best
of women. It was the knowledge that here at

home she was always praying for me that kept me from ruin in the hell in which I lived these many years. Surely they must have had another reason."

" Many things have happened since you went away last," replied the minister. " The people have all left the church they went to in your time, and the minister is dead. They meet now for worship two miles away; and Eachann Donn is their leader. Your mother was frail and not always able to walk, and she seemed to think I was kind to her, so she came to my church now and then. That was, I fear, the real reason."

Again the strong man was unable to control his emotion, and he said: "For ten years I have toiled, and my one thought was that I might come home to my mother again to make her happy and comfortable till she died. Many a night, coming home, I stood on deck listening to the throb of the engines, thinking each throb was bringing me nearer the moment when I would steal in at the gloaming and say

' Mother,' as I used in the old days—till I could feel, out there in mid-ocean, her hands going round my neck. And this is the end of it all!"

And he flung out his hands in an attitude of utter dejection and misery.

"She was the godliest woman I ever knew!" he exclaimed, as he was going out into the night " and they killed her!   I will never enter a church again!"

And he never did.   He stayed a fortnight with one of his brothers; but the two Sundays he was in Dunaluin, though there were four places of worship to choose from, where there used to be only two, he refused to go to any. He spent the days among the hills, and at the fortnight's end he left.   He was a wanderer, he said, and now he could not stay.   On the day he drove off to Dunskiath the wind drove the rain from the sea in blinding showers, and through the mists he passed to return no more. After a year had gone, word came that Alastair MacRaild had died of fever on the Rand.

IAN DUBH AND THE WIDOW:

IAN DUBH AND THE WIDOW

I

It was the immortal Sam Weller who used to get the affectionate advice from his father—" Sammy, beware of widders." There was a widow in Dunaluin, and the dimples on her cheeks when she smiled as well as said—" Beware of the widow." So thought the schoolmaster that day when he met her on his way to see Calum Og. She was coming from the hill with a load of fresh-pulled heather; for in the late summer, when the men are away at the fishing, the women in Dunaluin make large stacks of heather for the winter bedding of their cattle. If you have ever seen a woman carrying lightly a load of heather you will kn͟o͟w how Peggy, the widow, looked that day ͟ Mr. Padruig met her. The load was hu͟ a rope round her shoulders; it was ov͟

179

head and curled round her cheeks—crimson-
bloomed heather.   There was crimson also on
her cheeks, flushed by the exercise and the
fresh wind of the hills.   Her hair was jet
black, and curled in little ringlets about her
brow.   Her eyes were bright, and when she
smiled on the schoolmaster she showed white
teeth, gleaming between full red lips.   She
had on a short drugget skirt, with a little jacket
of homespun, and her hands were busy knitting.   Mr. Padruig gave a little gasp (he was
very susceptible in his youth), and thought of
the poet's description of the girl tying up the
rose branch—" A sight to make an old man
young."   What would the poet have said if he
had seen Peggy with her face surrounded by
that halo of heather bloom, and her eyes lit up
with the brightness of the summer hills?   Padruig felt a little pity for the poet who had only
seen the fair one among the roses.   If he had
only seen her with a load of heather!

Calum Og lived in the house next to the
widow's on one side, and Ian Dubh occupied

the croft on the other side. Ian Dubh was a
bachelor who had an old aunt keeping his
house. That day when Mr. Padruig reached
Calum Og's house he found Calum sitting on a
sunag at the side of his door in the sun. A
sunag is a low chair made of plaited straw with
back-rest and arm-rests. When you sit down,
it closes up right round you. It seems to know
the muscles that are tired, and leans up gently
against them. A pipe and a sunag and a glowing peat fire, that was the height of bliss for
Calum Og. None of your morocco-covered
armchairs, thank you—they are nothing to a
sunag!

Well, the old man was sitting in his
sunag watching the cloud effects on the sea,
and Mr. Padruig sat on a stone beside him.
As he sat down they saw the widow depositing
her load of heather at the end of her house.

"Isn't the widow looking well?" said the
schoolmaster to Calum.

"That she is," said Calum, "and little wonder; she brings home a load of heather every

day! But I am thinking she is not going to be a widow very long."

"Who is the man?" queried the schoolmaster, a trifle eagerly.

"Have you not heard," answered Calum, "that she and Ian Dubh, whose croft is beside hers on the other side, are to be married when he comes home from the fishing?"

"Are you sure you are right?" asked Mr. Padruig. "The widow is ten years older than he is, at the very least."

"I am sure of it," replied the old man from the depths of the sunag, "for Ian had a talk with me about it. Ian is a relative of mine— his mother was the cousin of the man who married my wife's sister—quite a near connection, so Ian naturally comes to me for advice. The widow is well-to-do. When her husband was drowned through the breaking of a rope on the steamer he was working in, she got a hun'red poun's compensation; and she has two cows and an old mare. Well, Ian came to me one night, and when he was sitting comfortably in this sunag with his pipe going well, he said to me suddenly:

" ' Calum,' says he, ' what do you say to my marrying the widow?'

" ' Man, Ian,' says I, taken aback like, ' she is ten years older than you.'

" ' But she has a hun'red poun's,' says he.

" ' She has three children,' says I; ' and how will you like to be rearing three children that are not your own?'

" ' They will be as useful to me as if they were my own,' says he; ' an' they are half-reared already.'

" ' Man,' says I at last, ' how will you like to go to church with an old, gray-headed wife twenty-five years after this, when you will be almost as fresh as ever? She will be sixty when you are fifty.'

" ' Calum,' says he, quite angry like, ' do you know how much money I get out of my croft every year? I'll tell you, if you don't. I sell a stirk every May for t'ree poun'; that's about all I get out of it. At that rate it will take me

thirty-three years and three months to make a
hun'red poun's out of my croft. Peggy has a
hun'red poun's, and by marrying her, I am
calculating I will be saving the work of thirty-
three years and three months. Just think of
that, you old dotard,' says he.

"Shortly after that," continued Calum,
"Ian Dubh and the widow settled it. He took
me with him to see the widow one night.
There was an old fence between the two crofts,
which was a cause of much dispute between the
two of them as to who was to repair it when it
broke down. The fence was broken at the
time. After a long *ceilidh*, Peggy said to Ian
that it was his turn to mend the fence this time.

"'Peggy,' says I, 'it would save a lot of
trouble if Ian and you did without the fence
altogether.'

"'What do you mean, Calum?' says she.

"'I mean,' says I, 'that if the two crofts
were thrown together there would be no more
need for the fence.'

"'How that?' asked she with her eye lighting up.

" ' How dense you are to-night, Peggy,' says I. ' If the two of you married there would be no more need of the fence.'

" She looked intently at the red peats for a little, while Ian Dubh breathed hard.

" ' I am quite agreeable,' says she at last.

" ' Then,' exclaimed Ian, ' we won't mend that old fence any more.'

" That settled it! and the old, out-at-elbows fence will never be repaired again," concluded Calum; " and they are to be married when Ian Dubh comes home from the fishing."

Then they began to talk of other things, while Calum smoked his bogie-roll, and Mr. Padruig sat wondering whether the day could come when he would attain that height of excellence—the smoking of bogie-roll. As he walked home to his solitary house, he carried with him the picture of the widow smiling at him from beneath the halo of crimson heather. It was as well, perhaps, that Ian Dubh was to marry her!

II

THE summer passed; the fishermen came home; the corn was cut and housed, and the potatoes pitted. That is the time of year when the sound of the pipes at a wedding is usually heard in Dunaluin. If you ask a man who is thinking of getting married when it is to take place, "When I will lift the potatoes," he will say. And yet, though the potatoes were lifted, there was no word of the widow and Ian Dubh getting married. That surprised everyone very much, and Mr. Padruig, one day he was seeing Calum Og, led up to the matter of the marriage.

"When is the widow's wedding to be?" he asked between whiffs of his pipe.

"Ach, master," replied Calum, "but that is a history by itself. Did you ever hear what Seumas Ruadh said to the minister when Seu-

mas was taking the marriage vows? No!
Well, I'll tell you. Seumas Ruadh was a bit
foolish; the *uisge-beatha* was his enemy, and
Seumas was a real Christian in this respect that
he loved nothing so much as his enemy. Once
the minister coming home late from the Presbytery found Seumas lying on the roadside, and
the minister never forgot it against Seumas.
At last Seumas thought he would turn over a
new leaf, and made up his mind to get married.
The minister, when he was tying the knot for
Seumas, thought it a good opportunity to rub
his duty into him. So he lectured poor Seumas
strongly on the evil of his ways; on the terri-
ble judgment that would befall a man who
would bring shame and sorrow on a woman;
on the great responsibilities that a man in-
curred when he linked another life to his own
in that he had to answer, not only for what he
had made of his own, but also what he made
of her life. (Ah! that was the right sort of
minister, said Calum, in an aside. He gave
it to the sinners. The young minister we have

now—he is a nice man, but he is soft. He goes on with bits of poetry, as if bits of poetry would ever put the tremors down the back of an old sinner like Seumas Ruadh.) Well, Seumus Ruadh caught it that night. At last the minister's breath gave out, and he turned to Seumas and asked him very gruff-like— 'Will you have this woman to be your wife?'

"By this time Seumas was white, and he looked up sideways at the minister.

"'Weel, minister,' says he, after a pause, 'after what you have said, I am just hoverin'.'

"And that's how it is with the widow and Ian Dubh just now," said Calum, applying his anecdote to the case in point. "The truth is that Ian Dubh is at present hoverin'."

"Hovering!" exclaimed Mr. Padruig. "Why, I thought he was very keen to get the widow and her hundred pounds."

"The hun'red poun's," echoed Calum, chuckling. "You have just hit it. But that's where the shoe pinches. Ian has found out that she has only fifty. You see, she was fool-

ish enough to sign a bill for her brother-in-law
last spring for fifty poun's. He was to buy a
big fishing-boat, and to pay the bill at the end
of the fishing season. It was difficult for
Peggy to refuse him. The money came to her
by the death of the man's brother. He made
sure he would meet the bill, but the fishing
failed, and the widow had to pay the bill, so
she has only fifty left. So Ian is hoverin' as
to whether it is worth while marrying her now
when she has only the income of a croft for
sixteen years and eight months, instead of
thirty-three years and four months, as she had
when he asked her. Isn't it a ticklish point for
Ian?"

And Calum chuckled deep in his throat
while he cut some bogie-roll with a rusty
knife.

"It is indeed a ticklish point for a mean man
like that," replied Mr. Padruig. "What will
happen now?"

"Ah! The widow," murmured Calum,
lighting his pipe with a glowing bit of peat;

"you trust the widow. She will soon bring Ian to his senses."

And so it turned out. The widow proved herself more than a match for Ian. She had an uncle who had lost a leg at the railway. When anything like that happens to a man in Dunaluin he invariably starts life as a merchant. The widow's uncle came home with a wooden leg, and in a corner of his barn he started a shop, where he sold everything from tea and sugar down to sheep-dip, paraffin, and tar. Tearlach Crubach (lame), as he was now called, soon proved that a man with one leg could be more prosperous than a man with two. Ian Dubh was much in Tearlach's debt, and, as he came home from the fishing poorer than he went, he was unable to pay. The widow waited on her uncle, and the uncle waited on Ian Dubh. Tearlach was a man with a hooked nose, flashing black eyes that looked through you, and a sharp tongue, and when Ian saw him coming in, his heart failed him. Like a greater man, Tearlach used great plainness of speech at that interview. He told Ian that he was the meanest man in Dunaluin, unworthy of the notice of an honest man, and that unless he fulfilled his word to the widow he would be sold out of house and stock for the payment of his debts. Ian Dubh quaked under the gleaming black eyes of Tearlach, and protested that he was an honorable man. The following Sunday Ian Dubh and the widow were proclaimed in the church.

The following Thursday the marriage took place. Usually in Dunaluin the happy couple head a procession to the manse, with the skirl of the pipes and the inspiring sounds made by a gun fired with blank shot each few hundred yards. But Ian struck at that. It was bad enough to marry a widow—a widow ten years older than himself—but to be marched through the parish to be made a spectacle of in the wake of the widow—no, he wouldn't! He waited on the minister; what arguments he used are not known, but at any rate he prevailed on Macleod (who was young and kind-hearted, as

Calum Og said) to brave the perils of a ride through the boggy township to Peggy's house. Among the guests assembled in the widow's kitchen were Calum Og and Mr. Padruig, and they watched the scene from a corner. Many a time afterwards did the schoolmaster tell the tale. There was a big glowing fire at the side of the room under the black hanging chimney made of wood, which caught the reek in its cavernous mouth. Two candles lit up the room, and in the dark corners barrels and nets loomed strange and mysterious in the shadows. The minister came and took his place with his back to the glowing *griosach*, and before him stood the marriage party. Near the window stood her uncle, Tearlach Crubach, balancing his wooden leg. The service began, and the widow looked as cool as if she were standing to be measured for a new dress; but Ian had a cowed look, and he was quaking with nervousness. The minister's address was full of the praises of love, and it sparkled with poetry; but the more Macleod waxed eloquent over the

immortality of love, its blissfulness and restful-
ness; over the watchfulness necessary for pre-
serving its tender bloom, the more restless grew
Ian Dubh, while the eyes of the widow sparkled.
At last the address ended, and the momentous
question was put—" Will you take this woman
to be your wedded wife?" At that moment,
as ill luck would have it, the widow's youngest
child uttered a scream from the bed in which
she was put away. At the sound Ian started as
if a knife were put into him. The scream grew
louder, and Ian said never a word, but stood
like a man transfixed. Then the minister began
the question again in a voice quavering with
nervousness. But still Ian Dubh stood as a
man who had lost his speech, and there was no
sound heard but the voice of the woman who
was trying to soothe the child. Then another
sound was heard, the tap, tap of Tearlach's
wooden leg as he quickly changed his place
to get his eyes full on Ian Dubh. Tap,
tap went the wooden leg till Ian at last saw
the glowing, piercing, threatening eyes of

Tearlach fixed on him. Then he found his voice.

"Of course, Mr. Macleod," he said. "Of course! What else?"

That was the end of Ian Dubh. It is strange how that little breath turns a man's life upside down. Before it is uttered a man is his own; after it, he is embarked on another sea, and not all the king's horses and all the king's men can bring him back to where he stood ere he uttered it. Doubtless that thought flashed through Ian when he heard the scream, and a dim hope dawned on him that it might not yet be too late—a hope which did not survive the tapping of Tearlach's wooden leg.

Ian Dubh's day was over from that night. In Dunaluin the wife is always known by having her name coupled with her husband's. When the husband rules, the husband's name is in the possessive case. There are exceptions in which it is the wife's name which is in the possessive case. Ian Dubh and the widow proved to be one of the rare exceptions. He

became known as Ian Dubh Pheggie—Peggie's black John.

When Mr. Padruig tells the story (which he
only does when he has sat a few hours in a
sunag and smoked many pipes) he always ends
by saying:

" The last time I met Ian Dubh I asked him
how his wife was.

" ' Oh, fine; Peggy is fine,' he answered; and
with a twinkle in his eye, he added—'She is at
present thinking it out as to who her third man
is going to be.' "

CALUM OG

CALUM OG

I

IT was on an evening in early spring, many years ago, that I first met Calum Og. The next house I was to call at, so they told me, was that of Calum Og, and from his name I naturally thought that I would find a man in the first flush of youth. When, however, I drew near to his door, an old, old man stood there, with a face lined deep and wrinkled, shading his eyes with one hand while he intently watched the steamer that was making its way out of the loch, heading across the Minch. Out of the door in which he stood there came curling wreaths of peat reek, for the house had no chimney, and the smoke from the fire that burned on a raised stone hearth in the center of the earthen floor made its way out through a hole in the roof in which a bottomless creel was fixed, and through the door.   The evening was still; the smell of the new-turned soil was in the air; the sea was motionless and deep blue, save for the long trail of white foam in the wake of the churning steamer; while, over the bold headland of Dunskiath, light, fleecy clouds, touched with gold, were fading into gray with the failing of the light. The glamour of the scene possessed me, and as I looked from the old man who stood framed in the eddying peat reek to the great boat that sped on without wind or tide, which he was gazing at with faded eyes, he seemed as if he were the spirit of his race—a weary, jaded spirit, coming forth for a moment from the shadows to look with melancholy eyes at the great world's triumphant progress, and then turing again to its own twilight dimness to gaze at the embers of dying fires, seeing visions of a dead past and of a fading present. Could this old man be Calum Og?   In the Isles, as I afterwards learned, it is not uncommon to find two sons in the one family called by the same name, and the

younger is always distinguished from the elder
by the epithet Og (young). Frequently it
happens that the distinctive adjective is used
when the need for it is long past, and a man
old and bent with the weight of fourscore
years is often known through the countryside
as Og. Thus it was with the old man who
courteously stood aside and invited me to enter
his humble abode.

"Did you see her?" he asked, as we sat by
the peat fire, which glowed red in the midst of
the heavy clouds of smoke that filled the house;
"the smoke-boat (*bata-na-smuid*), the hideous
thing! Well do I remember the first one that
came round Rhu-hunish. It was many years
ago, in the days of my youth, that one evening
I was out in a boat with an old man setting
fishing-lines. I rowed while he served out the
hooks and bait, when all of a sudden I saw the
lines drop from his hand, and his eyes staring
wildly as one that sees a bochan (ghost).
Turning to look in the same direction, I saw
a sight which turned my blood cold. Round

the Rhu there was coming towards us a monster craft without any sails, belching out smoke and flashes of fire from a red chimney, and as I looked it gave a scream which could be heard for miles. 'Cut the lines,' I cried when the first horror passed and I found my tongue again, and he cut them with trembling hands. Seizing one of the oars he pulled one side and I the other, making for the shore as quickly as ever we rowed in our lives. In the darkling eve we sat on the shore and watched the awful thing pass into the night. I never see that smoke-boat coming or going but I remember the first sight I saw of one coming round Rhu-hunish, when in our terror we cut our lines and fled. How I hate the sight of her!"

"But think of the great good the steamers have done to these lonely Isles," I said, remonstrating with the ancient man.

"Good!" he cried, with a flash in his eyes, which showed that, so far as his spirit was concerned, he was still rightly called Og. "Where is the good they have done? They have been the ruin of the Isles. In my young days every district had its own vessels—smacks and schooners—trading with the south. Can you see to-day any brown sails filled with the west winds passing south, laden with fish and eggs, or coming north, bearing the merchandise of the towns? No! The smoke-boats have done away with them all, and taken the meat from many a poor man's mouth. They have emptied the Isles. Each week the scream of their whistle seemed to say, ' Come with us and see the world,' and week by week the strong passed south. How many of them returned or saw the heather-clad hills again, or heard the waves beat on the shore? Look at the silent glens; the smoke-boats emptied them. They tell me that in the towns the people are packed, family above family, just as we pack herrings in a barrel. They never see the blue sky, or feel the sweet air with the smell of the heather, or lie on grassy mounds in the hearing of running brooks—a white and feeble folk! That is what the smoke-boats have done.

They have emptied the dales where strong men were reared, and filled narrow streets where men decay."

"You forget," I answered, "that the steamers bring men to the Isles as well as take them away."

"But what sort of men?" replied Calum; "only people who come for curiosity—tourists they call them. They never stay, that is one good thing; for they do nothing but harm. They corrupt the people. They come with their grand airs, employing guides, and ghillies, and waiters, and have turned kindly men into greedy expectants of shillings and half-crowns. When I was young people helped each other out of the kindness of their hearts, but now nothing is done for the man who has no money. The old kindliness is gone, the smoke-boats have killed it. A curse on them, say I."

II

As the year advanced, and the braes sloping
down to the sea began to rustle with the growing corn, I went often of an evening to see
Calum Og. His chief occupation was tending
his cow as she grazed on the patches of sweet
grass between the corn-ricks. He was always
to be found near sunset, standing between the
browsing beast and the growing crop, intently
watching the lengthening shadows on the
Sound. He had a weakness for very strong
black tobacco, and whenever I brought him that
luxury and he settled to the enjoyment of his
pipe, sucking it with a puckered face which
threw all its deep lines into relief, he would
speak with loosened tongue of the things that
were long, long ago, ere the smoke-boats came
defiling the lochs or the scream of the iron
horse was heard, or so much as dreamt of, at
the narrow Kyle. When I had come to know

him well, I asked him one evening how old he
was.

"My years are many," he answered, "but
their number is what I cannot tell. It is weari-
some waiting for their end; and I am afraid it
will not come yet a while, for you must know
that Death has forgotten me."

"Forgotten you, Calum!" I said, startled;
"that is impossible. Death never forgets, and
comes always at its own set time."

"So they say," he replied, with a shade of
sadness and humor in his deep-set eyes like the
mingling of rain and sunshine on the hillside;
"but I tell you I am alive to-day because Death
must have forgotten me. If you wish I will
tell you the way of it."

"Do tell me," I said eagerly, prepared for a
curious fancy.

"This is how it happened," he resumed.
"Though I have lived here since before the
famine, when the potatoes failed, and the people
lived a whole summer on the shell-fish they
gathered on the shores at the ebb-tide and on

blood they drew from their living cattle, yet I do not belong to this place. I belong to another district—a parish in Trotternish, across the loch. All my brothers are dead long ago; their children are now old men and women; and I, the only one who left Trotternish, am still alive. It often comes over me that I am left because I came away from my own place. When Ian, the last of my brothers, died, I often think that Death must have said to himself—' I have taken the breath from all Domhnull Ruadh's children now, and gathered them all to their lair side by side '; but he forgot me for these twenty years now, because I left Trotternish. I am thinking I must go back to the old place ere he will remember me."

And the old man gazed along the pathway of silver that stretched across the shimmering Minch towards the setting sun.

" Were the others old when they died ? " I asked, wondering at the ancient's fancies.

" Old! They were not old," he answered, speaking slowly as one recalling half-forgotten faces. "At least not what I would call old. Some saw sixty, and some seventy summers— but that is not old. Death knew where to find them when their time was run. The one who lived longest of our race was my grandfather." With that there came a look of lively recollection into the dim eyes, and he exclaimed—"My grandfather saw the Prince. Did I tell you that story?"

"The Prince! What Prince?" I asked. "No, you did not tell me."

" There is only one Prince spoken of in the Isles," he answered, with an almost angry flash. "But I forgot; how could you know of the Prince with the yellow hair?—*a Prionnsa Tearlach.* Many a time did I hear the tale from my grandfather when I was a boy in the days of long ago. The shadows were gathering when the boat that bore the Prince and Flora from Uist passed the Rhu out there. The Macleod Militia (Macleod did not side with the Prince, but with King George) lined the shore behind the rocks, and fired a volley at the passing boat, but not a bullet came near them. Instead of landing as they intended, they made for Trotternish. My grandfather was a servant with Macdonald of Kingsburgh, and he attended his master that day on a visit to Lady Margaret at Mugstod. When the boat got to the shore below Mugstod, Flora at once waited on Lady Margaret, and told her the Prince was on the shore. The lady, in great distress, for King George's soldiers were in the house, took Kingsburgh into her council.

He at once sent my grandfather to the shore to tell the Prince to hide behind the big rocks lest the soldiers should see him. The Prince was sitting on a rock when my grandfather reached him. He was dressed like a servant maid with a loose, flowered linen gown, a white apron, and a currachd (cap) on his head. But under the currachd the yellow hair curled round his brow, and his face was so fair that the messenger, struck with awe, fell on his knees, saying:

" ' Your Highness, Kingsburgh sent me to tell you to hide behind the big rocks yonder.'

" ' That is well,' he answered, and before the other rose off his knees the Prince was over the rocks, tucking up his gown as he ran."

" But, Calum," I said, " I remember reading in a book that it was Neil MacEchan whom Kingsburgh sent to the shore—the same Neil who followed the Prince to France, and was the father of the great Marshal Macdonald, Duke of Tarentum."

" What! " exclaimed the old man impatiently; " you seem to know much about it. You read it in a book, did you? Do you not know that books are lies—nothing but lies? There used to be no books and no papers in the Isles, and men spoke the truth then. Now they come to every house, and one hears nothing but their lies every day. I tell you it was my grandfather who was sent to the shore, and he never told the story of how he found the Prince sitting on a rock in a flowered gown, eating dulse, without dropping the salt tears as he told it. But if you know the tale, then I need not go on."

"Oh, go on, Calum," I said, feeling I had blundered.

"Well, then, but don't tell me about your books!" he resumed; "and I will finish, seeing I began. When they decided what to do, Kingsburgh himself went to the shore to take the Prince with him, but he could not find him anywhere. At last he saw the sheep in a little dell restless and running about, so he knew someone was there. When he reached the spot the Prince sprang up ready to defend himself, not knowing but it might be an enemy; but Kingsburgh exclaimed—' I am Macdonald of Kingsburgh, come to serve your Royal Highness,' and bending on one knee he kissed his hand as if he were in his palace, and not disguised as a servant-maid hiding among the sheep. After he explained to the Prince what was decided on, they started for Kingsburgh. My grandfather, and a serving-maid who was going to Kingsburgh, walked behind them, and when she saw the Prince lift up his skirts too high when passing the rivers (there were no bridges then), she whispered to her companion —'What a shameless hussy that is. She must be either an Irishwoman or a man in woman's clothes.' My grandfather assured her she was an Irishwoman. That night the Prince slept in a bed with linen sheets, as he had not done for months. Years afterwards, Mrs. Macdonald of Kingsburgh was buried at her own request with her body wrapped in the sheets in which her Prince slept. Ere he left in the morning he put his head in Flora's lap, and she cut off some of the golden curls. Gold would not buy these locks of hair from those who received them. Many a man has looked at them since through tears. Kingsburgh gave the Prince a new pair of brogues when he left, and taking up the old tattered pair he said:

"'I will bring these and throw them at your Royal Highness's feet when you are at St. James'.'

"'Do,' answered the Prince, 'and I will know how to reward you.'

"And so he passed, and my grandfather saw him no more; but often he would say when he told the tale that the Prince would come back again. Do you think he will?"—and with a far-away look of infinite sadness the old man's voice faded into silence.

"He cannot come back; he is dead long ago, as you know," I answered.

"Dead long ago!" the old man murmured; "so he is! Kingsburgh, and Flora, and Lady Margaret, and all who loved and served him are dead. The glens are wrapped up in silence, and the sea is moaning for them that are no more."

A tear was on his furrowed cheek as I bade him good-night, and as I wandered home through the fast-falling darkness I thought of the deathless love wherewith these men loved their Prince. Poor men all!—and though one word of treachery would make him who spoke it rich beyond the dreams of Hebridean avarice, there was none found to speak that word. He passed through these lonely Isles, where the wind and the waves and the rain sing their melancholy dirges—weary, ragged, woebegone, with his hopes drowned in blood—a figure so pathetic that one can hardly look at him without tears even across the long years; and yet, was it not in victory he passed, conquering human hearts in which he will reign forever, crowned with a love that will never fade? Dead! no; for love and devotion such as theirs will never die. Calum Og might have said with truth that Death had forgotten them.

III

WHEN the corn had been gathered home, and the potatoes had been covered from the frost in two long pits before his door, and the big stack of peats at the end had been securely turfed, and the heather ropes on his house had been well mended and tightened, then Calum Og became restless. One night in the beginning of winter I found him sitting as usual in the midst of clouds of peat reek, watching with a wistful look the hollows that flared red in the center of the hearth, doubtless seeing in the red embers visions of the days that are no more.

" I was thinking," he began musingly, " that I will be stepping over to Trotternish before the winter sets in. I have not been there these long years, and I am thinking that if I go to the old place, Death will remember that he has not brought me home yet."

"You are talking foolishness, Calum," I replied, "for Death never misses anyone. There are many who wish he would."

"That may be," he said; "but I have taken a great longing to see the old place I played in as a boy. When I was a lad I remember hearing an old minister with white hair, preaching about a king who, when he was worn and thirsty, called out for a drink from the well that he drew water from as a boy. Do you know the words?"

"It was David," I replied. "When he was weary with the battle and thirsty with the heat he cried—' Oh, that one would give me to drink of the well of Bethlehem which is by the gate!'"

"These are the words," and the old man repeated them. "I remember them as one remembers things he has seen in a dream. There was no water so sweet to the king as the water he drew in his youth, and I am yearning to taste again the water of the well of my youth. The house where I was born is a *larach* (desolate), but the well is flowing there still."

Shortly thereafter, when, as I often did, I made my way in the gloaming to Calum Og's house, I found that he had on that morning gone on his pilgrimage to the scenes of his boyhood. There was a cart going to Port-a-Righ, and Calum went with it to the head of the loch that winds in among the hills. From there he was to walk to the house where he meant to stay, and the road led him through the township which he knew of old, whence the people had been removed to make place for sheep. No curling wreaths of smoke rising from warm thatched houses gave a look of cheerful life to the lonely place; no sound of human activity broke the stillness; and the laughter of children at play, which the old man seemed to hear in the gathering gloom, was only the memory of what was fourscore years ago.

Slowly, 'mid the grassgrown mounds which marked the foundations of the houses he knew, the old man made his way to the well whence he had so often drawn water for his mother in the days long gone. It flowed as of old, but the heather was now growing round it. He was tired with his long journey, and he sat down after he had slaked his thirst. The keenness of the winter's first frost was in the air, heavy clouds came sailing in from the sea, and a few flakes of snow fell fluttering to the ground before the west wind. The head of the way-worn pilgrim fell on his breast as one who is falling asleep. Raising himself, he suddenly cried—" I am coming, mother," for it came to him that he was a boy again loitering with the pitcher at the well, and that his mother was calling him. But again the head nodded on his breast, and he fell fast asleep by the well of his youth. In the morning they found him there, with a light coverlet of glistening snow drawn over him. " Death from exposure " they called it, but it seemed to me as if Death had remembered Calum Og just when he returned to the place of his youth, and had at once led him gently from the fitful slumbers of time to the deep unbroken sleep which is now his, as he lies with the dust of those he loved in the little churchyard, by whose side a river flows, in Trotternish.

THE SHADOW OF A CREED

THE SHADOW OF A CREED

I

IN a little hollow beside the sea, in the midst of the parish's dead, stands the parish church of Skerra. They called it the Church in the Clachan, because a little cluster of cottages stands near it. Southward the beetling crags overhang the little village, and behind these · there stretches a wide district, untenanted save by grouse and deer. In the autumn the sound of guns comes over the cliffs, and then the cottagers know that the sportsmen have come to the wilderness, and they wonder in a dull way who these strangers are. To the north lies the great North Sea, that even on still days breaks with a dull, rhythmic sound upon the stretches of sand and jutting rocks that form the coast-line. This little hollow is the loneliest of places; for no ship can anchor off these inhospitable shores, and the road that skirts the coast-line runs for forty miles ere it comes to a town. The necessaries of life come hither in strange ways. Many, many years ago a great ship was driven by the autumn gales on these shores. One by one, till none remained, the sailors were snatched from the spars and dashed against the cliff by the remorseless sea; and they were reverently laid in nameless graves in the clachan. The roof of the church is made of the woodwork of that ship; and the ship-bell, hung above its door, now calls the people to prayer. On that day of death long ago, as the irresistible waves dashed over the doomed ship, the bell rang out its toll, and those on shore heard it above the blast. The cruel sea tolled it then; but trembling hands toll it now when the dead are brought and laid to rest around the weather-beaten church in the clachan.

To the west of the village that nestles in the hollow, on a hill stands the inn, which feels the flutter of life only once a day, when the blown horses drag the mail-car up the steep road that leads to its door, and a passenger or two descend to refresh themselves and to tell the world's news to the lonely dwellers on the hill. From its door one can see wondrous views of the sea that is never still, and of the great mountains to the south, between which there opens up a long valley, through which a river flows fringed with straggling birch 'mid green fields of loamy soil. Looking down from the height on the smoke-wreathed cottages, the gray-walled church in their midst, the sheltering hills and the glimmering sea beyond, it looks as if the spirit of unbroken peace brooded over the clachan.

So I thought on that summer day, when, an aimless wanderer, I alighted on the hill and stayed at the old inn; but I was not long there before I learned that the burdens of shadowed lives and sore hearts were here as well as in the restless city whence I came. The way in which that knowledge came to me I will now tell.

It was a hot, still, cloudless day—one of

those days on which it is useless to cast the flies on the lochs that lie bowered in heather among the hills. The inn was stifling, and I wandered down to the shore, where the stretches of sand were wet with the receding waves. On a sultry day a wave-laved beach is the coolest of places, and I stood there with great content, watching the lazy ground-swell curling in ridges of curds around the bay, till suddenly I heard a short, hacking cough coming from behind me. It was a discordant note breaking on the stillness, and I turned round to see whence it came; but I saw no one. After a little, when the wash of the cool waves at my feet had again stilled all my being, it came again from behind—that same short, choking cough. This time I walked towards the sand-banks that bordered the strand to see who was there. In a little hollow, with his back reclining on a sand-dune, basking in the heat, I came on a lad of some eighteen years, intently reading a dog-eared book. His face was so thin that the bones stood out prominently beneath

the white skin. His hair was ruddy, with
gleams of gold as the sun shone on it, curling
beneath his cap. His fingers were long and
wasted, and the nails, white and transparent,
bent over their tips. He rose as I came near,
but I asked him to sit still, and if I might sit
for a little beside him. To this he assented
with a quaint shyness.

"What are you reading?" I asked, by way
of opening a conversation. He handed me the
little brown-covered book. It was a school
edition of Tennyson, and was open at
"Œnone." I read aloud the matchless opening lines:

> "There lies a vale in Ida, lovelier
> Than all the valleys of the Ionian hills.
> The swimming vapor slopes athwart the glen,
> Puts forth an arm, and creeps from pine to pine,
> And loiters slowly drawn. On either hand
> The lawns and meadow ledges midway down
> Hang rich in flowers, and far below them roars
> The long brook falling through the clov'n ravine
> In cataract after cataract to the sea."

"These are the lines I like best," said the

lad in a dreamy voice, looking with a wistful gaze towards the glen where the river flowed into the sea. "It seems as if it were the strath up there, when the summer mists are rising upwards towards the sun, and the great hills, clothed in their shimmering drapery, stand sheltering it from the winds."

"Only there are no cataracts," I said.

"Neither there are," he resumed in a regretful voice; "but there are deep pools in which the shadows come and go, and the fields are full of buttercups and wild clover, and the heather gleams crimson and red on the slopes above, and the trailing mists are continually putting forth an arm, caressing it here and there."

He was no common lad who could speak thus, while his eyes lit up with the poet's fire in them as we talked of the great singer who had wedded thought and the melody of words in the little brown book I held in my hand. Here and there I read, and all I read was familiar to him.

The afternoon was creeping on, and a heavy cloud drifted between us and the sun. A breeze sprang up from the sea with the cold edge to it which is never lacking in the wind of these northern districts. The lad shivered, and a fit of coughing seized him which shook his frail body. When he took his handkerchief from his mouth, it was spotted with blood.

"I must be going home," he said; and rising up, he put the paper-covered book into his inner pocket as if it were the most precious of volumes, and walked off slowly over the stretch of sand which lay between us and the township where he lived. As he walked away from me, I noticed how loosely his homespun clothes hung on his wasted limbs.

After that day I often came upon the lad with his back to the wind and his face to the sun, reading in sheltered nooks beside the sea, and little by little I came to know his short life's story. His name was Alan, and he was the son of Padruig the shoemaker, whose house lay in the nook of the bay. Of all the stern

faces there to be seen in Skerra, Padruig's was
the sternest.   His eyes were narrow and had a
hard look in them.   His cheeks were covered
with iron-gray whiskers; but his chin and upper
lip were shaven, showing a determined mouth.
It was he who led the revolt in the congregation
that met in the church on the moor, when the
people took possession of the church and shut
their minister out.   Whereas the church in the
clachan was well-nigh empty, the church on
the moor was full; and Padruig was the leader.
There he took part in the service and ex-
pounded his doctrines.   Alan was Padruig's
eldest son, and never was son more unlike his
father.   He was a dreamy boy from his childhood, and his dreaminess gained him many a
beating.   Being the eldest in the family, the
duty of herding the cows in the evenings on the
sweet grass that grew between the corn-plots
on the croft fell to Alan; but often his mother
would come to the door with her hands white
with her baking, and she would see the cows
grazing in the midst of the corn, while Alan

would be standing motionless gazing on the
sky, where the clouds, like sheep-fleeces, were
coming athwart the setting sun. "Alan,
Alan!" she would cry; and Alan, descending
from heaven to earth, would rush to save the
corn. Mairi never reproached him more than
in the way she would call his name; but his
father, when he caught him dreaming and
the cows pasturing in the corn, used sterner
measures. The boy was supremely happy only
when he was reading. Books were, alas!
scarce in Skerra. Padruig's library consisted
of only "The Pilgrim's Progress," Boston's
"Fourfold State," and a few volumes of stern
sermons. Happily for the boy, he one day
discovered that there was a little library of
books in the vestry of the church in the clachan,
which some pious minister had put there. The
library was small: there were many theological
books in it useless to a boy; but there was also,
like an oasis in the wilderness, an old edition
of the Waverley novels. The books were to be
had for the asking, and Alan devoured them

one by one as he lay hid among the sand-dunes, unseen by his father. The world grew wide on his view as his body lay softly on the bent, and his spirit roamed through the realms of romance with princes and heroes and ladies of fair renown. Alan hid the books so carefully that it was only once the stern Puritan caught his son in the act. It was on a Sunday, and Alan was so absorbed in the weirdness of "Wolf's Crag" that the first sign he had of anyone near was his father's voice asking what he was reading on the Sabbath? The boy could not find a word to reply, and Padruig took the book from his hand. When its nature dawned on him, Padruig threw it down and stamped it into the sand with his heel.

"Where did you get it?" he asked in a stern voice.

"From the vestry in the church in the clachan," answered the trembling boy.

"A worthy place for such a book," exclaimed the irate Calvinist. "It is long since the Gospel deserted the church in the clachan; little wonder they have made it a storehouse for lying books!"

The next morning (for Padruig would not break the Sabbath by administering discipline) Alan received the last beating from his father. He was told he would fare much worse the next time his father caught him reading any more of the corrupting books from the church which the Gospel had deserted. But many beatings would not keep Alan from the books, which were to his thirsty spirit as the wells of Elim to the parched wanderers in the desert. He read on as before: only Padruig never caught him again.

Alan was now the best scholar in the parish school, and the old master spoke enthusiastically of his gifts to the young minister who preached in the church where the old ship-bell rang every Sunday, summoning a congregation that never came. "If he only had a chance, he could do anything," said the old man; and the minister resolved, if he could, to help Alan. Alan was asked to the manse, and the minister gave him books to read such as he had never dreamed of. Poets now sang to him by the sea; historians narrated to him the wonders of the ages; and the world grew, day by day, brighter and brighter for Alan the dreamer. Every evening he went to get lessons from his new friend, and he resolved within himself to become a minister also. Having already learned enough Latin to know that "all Gaul is divided into three parts," he attacked the outposts of Greek with a will.

It was the summer-time when these things came about, and Padruig was away in the south working till the time of harvest. At last the corn was turning golden in the fields that sloped down to the sea, and Padruig came home to the reaping. When he heard that Alan was going to the minister for teaching, he frowned; when he heard that Alan, in the gratitude of his heart, had been going to the minister's church and that sometimes Mairi had gone with him, he frowned deeper still. The

gentle mother praised the minister, and told
how kind he had been to Alan and to herself
when her child was ill. Surely it was not
wrong to go to his church!

" I will go there the first Sabbath, and judge
for myself," said Padruig. When Sunday
came, Padruig went with Alan to the old
church, within whose walls he had never worshiped before; but what he heard there was not
to his mind. The sermon was a tender, mystical sermon on the love of the All-Father.
Padruig waited eagerly for a distinction to be
drawn between the Father's love to His own
and His love to those outside His elect; but
the preacher only dwelt on the tenderness of
His love to those " out of the way "; for did
not the mother love all the more the child
whose frailties made the greatest claim on
her?

" He is not sound in the faith," declared
Padruig, when he got home. " We will not
go near the clachan church again."

Alan was forbidden to go to the manse any

more, lest he should be led away from the old paths. In vain did he rebel against his father's iron will. In vain did he plead that he might be allowed to go on preparing himself for going to college. His father apprenticed him to a stonemason.

It was little more than a year after Alan went away to learn his rough craft that he returned with the hacking cough which drew me to his side among the sand-hills. The hopelessness which gnawed at his heart was but poor armor against the exposure to wind and rain to which his work consigned him. His slender frame was not equal to the toil. When he came home, Mairi said he had come for a week, as he had a bad cold; but the neighbors, when they saw him, knew that he had come home to die.

Now Alan waited for the strength that would not return. On the cold days he crouched over the peat fire with his mother's plaid around him, and on the warm days he lay on the bent-covered hillocks and read. The last day I found him there he was watching a white-sailed brig sailing away towards the west.

"What do you think death is?" was his startling question, after we had talked a little.

I, who had never thought of the mysteries of life and death, who seldom went to church, and seldom prayed, who had thought life well spent if I could only get people to read the stories I tried to write—what answer could I give to the lad who stood in the valley where the shadows were already falling round him?

"I am afraid I cannot say," I answered lamely. "No man has seen death at any time."

"Yes, I know," he said. "We see only what death does. Look at that ship" (and he pointed to the white-sailed brig). "You see it disappearing, little by little, below the horizon. Soon it will be out of sight; yet, though it has entered what is for us the unseen, it is not sunk or lost. It is sailing on, perhaps to brighter shores. It may be like that with death. Perhaps death is only the horizon."

After that day I found him no more among the sand-hills that fringe the bay. I heard he had got worse, and then I heard he was dead. He had sailed beyond the horizon. As I was no longer a stranger to Mairi, on the day after Alan died I went to the house and asked if I might see the last of the lad I had learned to love. I was courteously asked to enter. On a bed in the inner room Alan lay, white and still, and the ruddy locks still curled round his brow. Padruig sat with bowed head beside the fireplace; the mother sat beside her dead son, and she was stroking his hair, while she kept murmuring to herself, " He is not dead; my beloved is not dead."

" No, Mairi," said the young minister, who had been Alan's friend, and who sat near her, " Alan is not dead; he has only entered into the fullness of life."

" You mean he has gone to heaven," she said eagerly. " If I were sure of that, I would be patient—oh! so patient."

" Yes, I mean that," he said slowly and tenderly. " Alan had great gifts, and God had a use for them elsewhere."

" And I was his mother," she said, with her eyes shining.

It was then that Padruig lifted his head, which had been buried in his hands. His face was drawn and haggard.

" Be quiet, wife," he said, in a voice gentler than was his wont. " Neither Mr. MacCormic nor anyone else can say how it fares with the dead. ' God has of His mere good pleasure elected some to everlasting life '; who these are God alone can tell. Poor Alan is in His hands; we can only submit to His will."

Mairi shrank at the words, as if a knife had pierced her. Her large eyes filled with hot tears, and the look of misery returned to them. She ceased stroking the head of her first-born, and sank deeper into her chair, sobbing.

The minister rose and went out into the sunshine, and I followed him. Neither was ashamed that the other saw him brushing away a tear.

On the next day they buried Alan in a corner of the churchyard, where the wind from the sea blows on his grave, and where the fine sand driven by the gale falls softly over him when the breakers dash up on the strand, and the north wind whirls through the clachan. An old man with a quivering face tolled the old ship-bell as they lowered him to his rest; the beetling crags echoed the knell, and across the field we could hear the sob of the sea washing the hollowed cliffs along the bay.

II

" THAT is poor Alan's grave."

The old man pointed to a slab of gray slate that stood erect in a corner of the churchyard in the clachan. It bore a name with some dates, and the words, " A place is vacant at our hearth which never can be filled." There was no sign on it of the hope of immortality or the resurrection from the dead. An ugly stone with an uglier epitaph!

" I could tell you many strange things about this place," resumed the old man; " but that stone has a story as sad as any I know. Would you care to hear it?

" You would like to hear about Alan, you say. He was the eldest son of Padruig the shoemaker, whose house lies in the loop of the bay over there. Padruig is the sternest man in Skerra—a truthful, honest, God-fearing man; but without any of the grace of tenderness. Alan took after his mother, and was a gentle, dreamy youth, who would sit contentedly a whole afternoon watching the clouds. Give him books, and a sheltered corner in the sun, and he was happy. He could have done anything if he only had a chance. He wanted to be a minister; but everything went against him. His mother loved him all the more because he never got his opportunity. Padruig apprenticed him to a mason, and a year afterwards he died.

"The snow fell early that year in Skerra. One morning in November the people awoke to find the world white, and the snow still falling softly in glistening flakes before the north wind. In the afternoon the sun shone out and lit up a transfigured world. The hills shone in the light, 'clothed in white samite, mystic, wonderful'; the sea was a mass of white, foaming waves, and round the shore the white spray leaped. Nothing but white was to be seen, save the blue of the sky between the clouds, and a stretch of sand left wet by the ebbing waves.

" Across that stretch of sand, when I moved out towards evening, I saw two figures coming towards the church, walking rapidly. They did not walk side by side, but one after the other. The woman in front moved quickly and unsteadily, while the other followed doggedly behind. I watched them till they disappeared among the sand-dunes that fringe the bay; I watched them again as they emerged and walked across the white field to the gate leading to the church. The woman in front had a black shawl drawn round her head, and she passed through the gate and walked between the snow-white mounds to the corner where Alan lay, and threw herself, face down, on the grave. Then I knew it was Mairi, Alan's mother, who had come hither partly to see the stone which was placed there the previous day, and partly because she could not rest for the thought that the first snow was falling on her first-born's grave. (Alan was a dreamer

and a poet because of his mother.) In a little
while the other woman came up and tenderly
lifted Mairi, and led her out through the gate
and across the field. Before they disappeared
among the sand-hills, they turned and looked
towards the church. They stood there a
moment with their backs to the foaming sea,
where the waves leaped angrily and hissed in
the teeth of the wind; the heavy clouds hung
above them, and the snow began again to fall,
while these two were alone by themselves in a
weird, shrouded world. When at last her companion turned as if to go on, Mairi suddenly
stretched out her hands towards the graves on
which the flakes were again softly falling.
That was the last appeal of the mother's heart;
these hands stretched out as if groping for the
fair-haired child that laughed and crowed in
them—yesterday, was it not?

" I think it was the epitaph," continued the
old man after a pause, " which drew Mairi to
the grave that day in an abandonment of sorrow. When Padruig spoke of getting a tomb-

stone, Mairi set herself to search for a text to put on it. At last she decided on the words 'Seek Him who turneth the shadow of death into morning: The Lord is His name.' But when she spoke of it to Padruig, he would not have it. It would be against his 'principles' to put a text of Holy Scripture over the graves of any save those whose piety was such that there could be no doubt of their salvation. To all her tears and entreaties he only replied that he would be true to his 'principles.' And he was true to his 'principles,' and the stone was erected as you see it; and Mairi saw it for the first time when she stole out and came hither through the snow that day.

" ' It will make no difference to Alan,' said a friend to whom Mairi had turned for comfort; ' it matters nothing to him now whether there be a text over his grave or not.'

" ' But it would make a difference to me,' she said, as she rocked from side to side in her misery; ' I would be almost happy if there were only a text on it ! '

"That was the only time she ever spoke of it," concluded the old man, shutting the churchyard gate; "but at that moment she looked as one into whose soul the iron had pierced."

STRUGGLERS IN THE MIST

I

DEFYING THE LAW

THESE were dark and troublous days in the winged, wave-embraced isle of the mist, when a poverty-ridden people, wearied of their hopeless lives, fought with the shadows of their own misery, knowing not what they fought. They only knew that their lot was hopeless and miserable. The townships were spread over the slopes of a hog-backed, brown hill, and the sea washed up to the doors of the mean rush and heather-thatched houses, where cracked windows and gaping doors told their own tale of wretchedness. The winter had been the severest for many years; day after day the bitter north wind had swept through the sound, driving the long hissing waves that ran straight before it from the icepack, and broke with

thunderous roar over the jagged coast-line.
In other years the boats went out day by day
and set the nets in the evening, and in the
morning they went out again and came back
with food from the sea; but all through these
weary months hardly a boat left the shore.
The previous autumn had brought rainy day
after rainy day, till the corn rotted in the fields
and the potatoes in the ground. Now the bitter
barren spring had come, and the children went
to school with bare feet and wan faces and
white lips. They did not, however, all go to
the school; for day by day on a little hill above
the road, from the top of which one could see
the wayfarers coming two miles away, two
boys stood watching with keen eyes the narrow,
switchback road. They waited there day by
day lest the officers of the law would come on
the township unawares with the mysterious
papers which, if once delivered, would drive
the hungry people from their woeful homes—
so they thought. Great in their eyes was the
power of the missives of the law!

The spring passed on, and the watchers on the hill saw no sign of coming danger. Some said the danger was over, and the lads might as well leave the hill; but the wiser ones counted up the time till the day that the unpaid rents came due again, and said, we will keep our watch till that day, and keep it they did. At last what they dreaded happened. It was a still day, and the sea in the sound was as glass. The tide was far out, it being the great spring tides, and all the men and women were round the shore cutting the palm-leaved tangles and the crunching dark sea-ware, piling it high in their boats, where it shone like a glowing mass of gems as the sun-rays played on the wet, trailing leaves. The motionless sea, with the shadow of a cloud over it here and there; the fringe of dull red tangles moving lazily with the tide, gleaming in the sun like a golden hem to a shimmering skirt worn by a queen; here and there a boat among the sea's golden fringe, where men and women plied their bent hooks and cut the ware, singing as they worked—such was the peaceful scene on which the watchers on the hill looked down that day. Neither they nor another will see that scene again, for the people of the sea-girt Isle no longer have a reaping of the sea-shores when the spring comes round.

Suddenly from the hill top there broke the blast of a ram's horn, blown loudly and eagerly. 'Again and again it rose, echoing weirdly from the hills. The singer in the boat that lay nearest ceased her song; the hooks raised for the cutting of the tangles paused in the air; every eye turned to the hill, and there a red shawl hung limp at the top of a high pole. That was the signal. Every boat moved to the shore, and stern-faced men and excited women climbed the steep slopes that led from the sea to the road. In a few minutes a crowd stood in the narrow place below the hill, waiting with tense eagerness the coming of the emissaries of the law. They had not long to wait; for in a little they came up the brae to the narrow place where the road was blocked by the throng. There were only two, the sheriff-officer and his assistant, and when they saw the stern faces that looked menacingly at them as they came on, they quailed.

"Is not this a fine spring day?" said the officer in an insinuating voice to Ian Lom, whom he knew well, and who was a relative of his own, as he came up offering to shake hands. Ian Lom kept his in his pockets.

"I am thinking," answered Ian, "that it is a black, wae day; for it could be no other when you come on an errand such as this. I will not give you my hand, not though you were my brother, till I know what has brought you this day."

"Aye, let him tell what has brought him!" cried many voices at once, crowding round.

"My duty brought me," answered the servant of the law; "and you need not be afraid. I have only to give some papers to four of you, one in each township. The rest I have nothing to do with. It is sorry I am, but I am but a servant and had to come."

"If you were a man," said Ian Lom, "you would have given up your place, before you would come with these cursed papers to your own kindred. If we let you give these to-day, it will be our turn to-morrow. Back you go, and my evil wishes go with you."

"*Mille mollochd ort*" (a thousand curses on you), cried an old woman, throwing a clod of earth, which struck the officer on the cheek. His assistant turned and fled down the hill, with a shower of pebbles falling about him. Blows fell like hail on the man of the law, who was hemmed in by the throng. One man laid hold on his coat, and rent it down the back. "Dook him! Dook him in the stream!" cried excited voices. "We'll teach him to come this way again."

"Hold! hold!" cried Ian Lom, jumping to his cousin's side. "We will do him no bodily injury, lest a worse thing befall us," and, breaking a way through the mob, he extricated the messenger-at-law, who, without a hat, and his coat in ribbons, ran down the hill after his companion—a sad and deplorable contrast to the spruce man who left the town that same morning.

They stood there a little while with their excitement fast cooling. The old woman who had thrown the clod prophesied evil to the fleeing man to the third and fourth generation. "Hold your peace," said Ian Lom; "I am thinking we have not heard the last of this yet. We better go back to look after the boats." So one by one they descended to the shore again. The tide had turned and was gently flowing up the beach with an almost noiseless ripple. The tangles and the ware were covered by the incoming sea and no more could be done that day. The boats were put at anchor till the full tide, when they would be beached and unladen of their wet cargoes, which were afterwards to be carried home in creels to be spread on the crofts. Thus, as an interlude in the cutting of the sea-ware, did the township of Trotternish come in conflict with the power of the law. The worm had turned at last!

II

THE MAJESTY OF THE LAW

It was a raw, cold night, ten days later, when eighty blue-coated, helmeted men assembled in the town square of Port-a-Righ. They had come from all quarters, and their object was to uphold the majesty of the law. The Shirra himself, all the way from Dunedin, was at their head as they marched out of the town, at two o'clock in the morning, for their eight miles' tramp to arrest the rioters. That tramp, tramp through the darkness, with the sough of the wind coming over the mountains driving a spurt of rain now and again into their faces, and the eerie breaking of the waves as the road hugged the coast-line, was weird indeed. There were no sentinels posted at night, and the townships slept peacefully, none so much as dreaming of the blue-coated host marching

upon them through the darkness. The first
streaks of dawn were in the east when the host
halted above the hut of the first of those whom
they had set out to arrest. Silently the hut
was surrounded, and at the repeated knock at
the door there came treading softly over the
straw (for the door led first to the byre) a girl
with bare feet and a shawl round her. Fearing
no evil, she half opened the door, and two burly
men pushed in, throwing her backwards into
the cow-stall, and rousing Seumas Ban in his
bed, told him to dress immediately, as he was
their prisoner. Seumas obeyed at once, and
the children, wakened in their sleep, filled the
place with screams and lamentations. While
this was happening detachments of the blue-
coated army surrounded other houses, and
altogether arrested six men. But, while this
was being done, messenger after messenger
went through the place rousing every house.
Ian Lom was not among those arrested, and
the messenger who roused him was sent to
summon the people to the Cumhag, a narrow

place through which the Shirra would have to retreat with his prisoners.

No general ever chose a better spot in which to act on the defensive than this spot which Ian Lom chose for giving battle to the Shirra. It was well called the Cumhag. The road, after winding round a small dell, comes to the face of a hill which falls sheer down to the sea, and through the face of this hill the road was cut. For ten yards or so the outer edge of the road overhangs the sea, so that if one slipped over the grassy turf wall, which was the only protection, he would be picked up a mangled heap on the shore. On the inner side the hill rose right above the road, not high, but steep. Thither from all quarters the people flocked in garments which showed the haste with which they obeyed Ian Lom's summons. Ere the Shirra had seized his six prisoners there was considerable delay, and Ian Lom had time to organize a reception for him in the narrow defile through which he had to make his retreat back to the jail where he was to lodge his prisoners. Huge bowlders of stone were quickly gathered together on the top of the hill, and there they waited, resolved to rescue the prisoners.

The day was now fully bright, and the rain clouds which hung over the mountain broke in blinding showers, which the bitter spring wind drove over the half-clad crowd on the hill till they shivered with the cold, wet to the skin. But in their excitement they hardly felt it, and they had not long to wait. Along the narrow road they soon saw the enemy come, four deep, with their prisoners in the midst, each prisoner handcuffed to two of the Shirra's men. On they came through the rain, tramp, tramp, while below them on the Sound the spindrift was rising in clouds before the wind. When the vanguard entered the narrow place a shower of missiles fell on them from the hill, and one huge bowlder rolled down with a thud and passed but a foot or two from the foremost, and fell with a roar on the shore below. " Halt! Halt!" rose the sharp command, and

retiring a little from the point of danger a con-
sultation was held. Then the prisoners were
moved forward nearer the van; and slowly
they moved on again towards the defile, but
another shower of stones stopped them. No
bowlder was rolled this time, for the danger
would be as great to the prisoners as to the
enemy. One of the prisoners was already
struck, and he cried out, "For God's sake,
throw no stones." The defenders of the pass
had then to change their plans, and the men
climbed down with staves and heavy sticks to
hold the pass. Again did the Shirra order an
advance, and this time with drawn batons the
blue-coated army rushed to the defile. There
the battle was joined; skulls were cracked,
limbs broken, and the yells of maddening pain
and the shouts of eager fighters mingled with
the hiss of the wind on the sea below. Holding close together, wielding their batons with
the regularity of threshers swinging their flails,
step by step the compact blue mass pushed on,
while on the hill the women rent the air with

their screams; and even they were not idle, for whenever they saw a chance they threw a volley of stones, aiming so as not to hit their friends. At last the Shirra was struck, and a dozen men charged up the hill to clear the stone-throwers away. But now the pass was almost won. The compact mass made way by its weight through the undisciplined throng, and at last burst through. "Double quick, march!" sang out the Shirra, and the defile past, they rushed through the little dell, with the way clear and the victory won, while Ian Lom was left to care for his wounded, bandage up broken skulls, and carry home fainting women, and do the best he could to cover a severe defeat. Two hours later the six prisoners were lodged in jail. The worm that had turned was trodden underfoot, and the Shirra wore a piece of sticking-plaster for some days as a memento of his victory.

The crowd on the hill, looking after the prisoners, standing there in the rain, were disconsolate indeed. Curses deep and loud rose on every hand. The enemy had made a night march on them; why should they not make a night march on the enemy? The prisoners would have to spend a night in the jail at Port-a-Righ ere they could be removed; why not storm the jail and rescue them? The blood of Ian Lom was throbbing with the excitement of battle, and as yet he would not accept defeat. Only two or three of his men were disabled; the rest could more than storm the jail. So they decided that towards evening they would meet again and march for Port-a-Righ. The Shirra had won by treachery; but let the Shirra look to it!

III

.WHEN Shine, Ian Lom's wife, had cleaned and pasted up the wounds in Ian's head, and heard from him the plan of campaign for the night, she was in sore distress, though she carefully hid that from him. She was a gentle little woman, who had married beneath her, as her friends said; and the friend she loved best on earth was the wife of the factor at Port-a-Righ. It was the factor who sent the officer with these ejectment writs, which he had carried back in the pockets of his tattered coat. The anger which the people cherished against him was only a trifle less than their hatred of the Shirra. What would happen to him and his wife if Ian Lom and his people stormed the jail, and perhaps attacked his house afterwards, Shine trembled to think. She passed the morning in an agony of doubt and fear. Her loyalty to her husband prompted her to do nothing; her love for her cousin—a remote cousin, but she was her friend—urged her to do something to warn her of the coming danger. Noon passed before she decided on action.

Shine had only one son living, for all the rest had died—it was the memory of these which gave the tender look to her wistful eyes. She determined to send the boy to warn her friend to leave the town. Filling a basket with new-laid eggs, she told William, her boy, to put on his kilt and his good jacket, as she was to send him on a message. When the lad came with his tartan kilt, and his yellow hair curling below his Glengarry bonnet, she kissed him.

" Willie," she said, " who gave you that kilt and sporran ? "

" Why, mother," replied Willie, " you know that well. It was the factor's wife. Why should you ask ? "

" Because I want you to go on a message

from me to her," replied Shine. " Now, listen to me, and do what I tell you. You are to take this basket of eggs and go to the town. If anyone meets you and asks you where you are going, you are to say that your mother sent you to sell these eggs, and bring her home some tea and bread, as her tea is all done. Watch when you are going into the town, and see if you meet Mr. Alastair or his wife, and say to them, when nobody is near, that your mother sent you to tell them, for God's sake, to leave the town to-night, as mischief was going to happen. If you do not meet them, after you have sold the eggs and brought the tea, you will watch an opportunity when nobody is looking, and steal into the house and give the message; but see you give it to nobody but to Mr. Alastair himself, or to his wife."

Again and again she made him repeat over to her the directions she gave him until she was sure he knew what he was to do, and, kissing him once more, she sent him off, and watched him with shining eyes as he went, jauntily carrying the white-covered basket, until he was out of sight.   Ian Lom was all this time asleep, for the Shirra broke in on his sleep last night, and he wanted to be fresh for the coming night, when he meant to break in on the Shirra's sleep.

The day had cleared up at noon, and the bright sun of the last week of April was shedding its glory over the hillsides as Willie trotted on with his basket to the town.   He was a bright-faced boy, who had lived through eleven summers, and he was solemn beyond his years. He liked it when he got his tartan kilt to wear (for it was not often), and he felt all the vanity of his race tingling in him as he mounted the steep braes on the hilly road.   Through the townships he went, looking not to right or left, till he got to the moor where the heather grew at the roadside, and then he slowed down.   A grouse flew up near him and went flying low, and he was tempted to look where it was to nest, but he remembered his message and went on. A curlew leaped up in the marsh far down,

and flew towards the high mountains with its
weird, shrill cry, and he stood to look after it.
Then once more he stood watching a pigeon
making for the hollowed cliffs where the waves
wailed up into the caves, and he wondered at
the flutter of its flying till he saw a hawk far
up, hovering above it. He wished he could
have killed the hawk; and then he ran on again
till he saw the big houses of the town in the
bend of the bay, with the tower on the wooded
hill. What was the tower for? he wondered;
did soldiers live there to protect the island?
He would ask someone. Then another thought
came to him. The big school at the outskirts
of the town would be closing soon, and if he
did not hurry the town children would be out
when he passed, and would mock him for
carrying a basket with eggs. He could hear
the mocking cries—" Look at the egg-wife!"
just as if they were already calling after him;
so he hurried, and did not draw breath till that
danger was past, and he found himself entering
the little town which was to him so great and

wonderful. As he looked at the big houses,
and the jail with the high wall round it (he
shuddered as he passed it), he wondered if
there were any houses in the world bigger than
these. He skirted the back of the town first,
so as to get used to the look of things. Ere
he turned into the main street, and as he
loitered round a corner mustering up his courage to enter a shop, he came face to face with
Mr. Alastair, who was walking slowly down a
side street with a little white thing in his
mouth, which he was smoking. (Afterwards,
Willie found out that the white thing was a
cigarette.) Thus he came to meet Mr. Alastair, but at the sight of him his wits forsook
Willie, and he stood staring and trembling with
nervousness till the other passed. How was
he to speak to him? The factor did not know
Willie, though Willie knew the factor (a cir-
cumstance which is not uncommon as between
the great and the small in this little world).
The lad turned back and followed; the factor
was now going slowly out of the town along

the back road, and up and down Willie looked, and there was none in sight. Then, with the courage of despair, he ran until he overtook the factor, and pulled him by the coat. Mr. Alastair swung round and faced him.

" Who are you? " he asked, looking at the eager face below the Glengarry bonnet.

" I am Willie, the son of Shine, the wife of Ian Lom," answered the boy in a quavering voice.

"Oh! you are, are you? " said the factor kindly, shaking hands with him very gravely. " I know your mother. You are a kind of relative of mine, too, are you not? "

" So my mother says," said the boy; " and she sent me with a message to you. She told me to tell you, for God's sake, to take your wife out of the town to-night, as there is danger near."

The boy spoke with a rush, in his eagerness to get the words out. A hard look came into the factor's face, and he seized the boy by the arm.

"What danger?" he asked.

"She did not tell me," said the boy; "I was only to say that there was danger near you."

"But you know; tell me."

"All I know," said the boy, wincing at the grasp on his arm, "is that I heard my father tell my mother that the men were to come to the town to-night to break open the jail."

Mr. Alastair loosed his grip on the boy's arm and said nothing. He took out a little white case, and took another cigarette and lighted it.

"By Gad, they are, are they?" he muttered to himself. "We will see strange things this night."

Then he looked at the ground again, thinking deeply.

"Gad, I have it," he cried, and he smiled at the boy. Again he searched his pockets and took out a shining half-crown, which he gave to Willie.

"Buy yourself something with that," he

said kindly; "and tell your mother that I will not forget what she has done to-day."

And turning on his heels he went back up the lane towards his house, smoking as he went. Willie turned up the side street towards the big shops, feeling that he could go any-where now, after having faced the factor; and as he went up the street he wondered what Mr. Alastair meant when he said, "Gad, I have it!"

In the biggest of the shops Willie sold his eggs, and bought the tea and the bread as his mother told him, and leaving the basket with his purchases in it until he was leaving for home, he went out to have a look through the town. He was glad to be rid of the basket, for he did not feel at ease carrying it about while arrayed in the grandeur of his kilt. It was with a feeling of great relief that he saun-tered up the street, looking at the shop win-dows. Descending the steep brae he went down to the pier, and he held his head higher as he went, for he heard one woman ask an-other at a door, as he passed, " Whose is that

bonny boy?" A steamer lay at the pier un-
loading a cargo, and Willie looked on at the
cranes, and the sweating porters, and the
strange ship which was so great. What was
the world like where it came from? "*Clydes-
dale,* Glasgow," were the words he read on the
stern. Was Glasgow as big as Port-a-Righ?
He would like to go with that ship to Glasgow and see the world. Then he turned up
the town again, and knots of men were standing about, talking eagerly. He stood near,
listening, and he could make out little of what
they were saying, save that at regular inter-
vals they cursed the Shirra, and hinted how a
ship's mast would soon drive in the door of the
jail. Putting his hands in his pocket he found
the half-crown, and went up the street, wondering what he would buy. He saw a window
full of pictures and books, and stood to look at
it. Then he made up his mind all of a sudden;
he would buy a book. So in he went.

"What can I do for you?" said the shopman, smiling at him.

"I want to buy a book," said Willie.

"What book?" asked the other.

That was a question wholly unexpected, and Willie searched his mind in vain to know what book he wanted to buy.

"How much do you wish to give for the book?" asked the shopman.

Willie placed the half-crown on the counter as a reply to that. Then the shopman looked at his shelves. In a moment he brought down a thick book with a picture on the cover.

"Have you read 'Robinson Crusoe'? No! Well, that's the book for you. Its price is three-and-six; but, as you are the first who ever came into my shop to buy a book without a name, I'll give you it for the half-crown."

And Willie went out happy, having bought his first book. It was the turning point in his life, though at the time he knew it not. With a penny his mother had given him he bought a bun, and having got his basket, into which he put his book on the top of the tea and the bread, he left the town. When he got to the quiet road he began to eat his bun with great relish. The shadows under the trees reminded him that he had stayed too long in the town, and he made haste to be over the moor before it was dark. From the town, as he hurried on, he heard the call of a bugle, and then a pibroch stole over the air, making his heart beat fast. As he turned a bend of the highway he stood still; for there, sauntering on before him in the middle of the road, he saw Mr. Alastair all alone, with little clouds of smoke rising above him. "He is smoking the little white things," said Willie to himself; "and how am I to get past him?"

IV.

THE STRATAGEM

THE factor walked very slowly, and Willie could not muster up courage to come up with him. A mile further on Willie's road branched to the left across the river, while the main road kept straight on. Willie thought that Mr. Alastair would keep on the main road, and that he himself would thus have the way clear to turn to the left whenever the cross roads were past. So he walked slowly after the factor, but when Mr. Alastair came to the cross roads he turned to the left into the branch road, and Willie saw that he must pass him after all. The evening was now near; and, much to Willie's horror, he saw a knot of men behind a wall on the top of the ridge across the river. The factor stood on the bridge for a little, looking down into the pool, watching

the trout. Willie sat down beside the road, waiting to see what he would do next. Again and again Mr. Alastair looked at the road towards the town, as if expecting something. The boy looked too, and round the bend he saw a gleam of red, and full and clear there came the skirl of the pipes. It was a marching tune the piper played, with strange quavers and trills that gripped the boy's heart. On they came, the piper in front with the streamers flying from his pipes. He could hear the thud, thud, of the regular beating of their feet as they came near. Wheeling to the left, they entered a park and drew up to drill. The factor, when he saw them in the field, crossed the river and went up the brae. After a little, Willie followed, and when he got to the top of the brae he found the factor standing alone with a big crowd of men opposite him.

" What has brought you here, men? " asked Mr. Alastair.

" We have come to release our comrades, Mr. Alastair," said Ian Lom, " that's what we've come to do; and ye know it now, if you didn't know it before."

Willie slunk behind the men, holding his basket so that all could see it.

"You are mad," said the factor; "it will be the sorriest thing that ever happened in the Isle if you try it."

"Mad! are we? Mad!" exclaimed Ian Lom; "if we are it is good reason we have for being mad. What have we been but as the beasts of the field, these many years past? Our land was taken from us" (and he pointed to the hill which had been converted to a sheep run), "our rents have been raised, we have been driven about at the whim of every ground-officer, our children have been half starved, and now, since we won't and can't pay your rents, you steal on us in the night, and carry us off to jail. Mad! starved children drive their fathers mad to look at them, and ours are starved. We have paid and paid, generation after generation, rents for the land; we will pay no longer; we have paid for it all already; did your master make the earth that he should grind our faces for it? No! The earth is the Lord's, and we have as much right to it as he."

"And the cattle on a thousand hills is His," said the factor quickly; " then your cattle is as much mine as yours. How would you like me to come and drive them off, saying I had as much right to them as you?"

The fervor of Ian Lom's eloquence died down at that thrust. But in a little he got his voice again.

" How dare you come here to meet us," he asked, " after what you have done to us? You, who were brought up among ourselves, to turn on us like this! Go back lest we throw you in the river."

" Mille mollochd air! " they cried. " To the river with him; the water will soon cool the devil in the red factor."

Mr. Alastair did not budge. He took out his white case, and as slowly as if he were at home, he took out a cigarette and lighted it.

The coolness of the man quieted them. Willie looked at him with wondering eyes. He always remembered the factor as he saw him that evening—a short, stoutly-built man, with a large head and curly fair hair, and eyes that gleamed and flashed as he looked at the men before him. His hand did not so much as quiver. "That's what I call a brave man," said Willie to himself.

When the clamor died down, Mr. Alastair began to speak again. "Listen to me, men," he said; "I became factor when there was none of these troubles, and you know that nothing I did was the cause of these troubles. I have dealt fairly by you. Now, when you stopped paying your rents, I had either to take action against you or to resign. I thought it would be the cowardliest thing in the world to throw up my post, and desert my master in his difficulties. What would you think of a sailor who deserted his captain when a storm was brewing? Well, then, I stuck to my post, and because I did so I took steps against you. It was the only thing to do; and my honor compelled me to do it. And I have come here to meet you to prevent bloodshed. Look down there" (and he pointed to the field where the volunteers were drilling); "these men have rifles and ammunition, and they are to defend the jail to-night. You have neither rifles nor ammunition. What can you do? If you attack the jail there will be many widows this night in the island, and many children crying in the morning for their fathers, who will never come back to them again. For God's sake, men, go home, and I will do my best for you."

Just then, away down in the park, the captain had almost finished his drill. The company were drawn up facing the river. Each man had been served with a blank cartridge, and at the command, "Fire a volley!" a sound as of thunder came up the valley and echoed among the hills. At the sound the men on the hill started and looked at one another.

"You hear that," continued the factor;

" these men are drilling at present. Judge for yourselves what you can do."

" I for one am going home," said Tormoid, the bard. Tormoid had made a song extolling the bravery of his neighbors. As he came with the rest that evening, he had been heard saying that, as he had almost killed a man that morning, he would not go near the jail that night lest he should be caught and hung; at which Ian Lom whispered to his neighbor, " The man never threw a stone." But the bard's task is not to do brave deeds, but to give the brave deeds of others immortality in song. It was, therefore, natural that Tormoid should be the first to say, " I am going home."

The rest, realizing the cause was hopeless, turned and followed Tormoid homeward through the fast-falling night. Ian Lom went last of all, and he shook hands with Mr. Alastair ere he turned and followed his men.

" Take a beannachd (greeting) from me to Shine," said the factor.

"That I will," said Ian heartily; "for whatever you are, you are at least a brave man."

And the factor turned townward, still smoking his cigarette, but with a sad look in his face. As he crossed the bridge he saw the lights from the town gleaming in the bay, and the wind blew chill down the valley. He had played a game of bluff, and he had played it well.

It was the drill season of the volunteers, whose colonel he was, and after meeting Willie he arranged with the captain that the latter would march the men that evening up the valley and have firing exercise in the field facing the hill road. He thought that in the dusk the men who meant to attack the jail would begin to gather there; and it was as he thought. As to the volunteers defending the jail, that was only a ruse on his part; but when he thought of the lives that would be lost ere the Shirra, with eighty men under him, would surrender his prisoners; of all the misery which would follow after that,—the imprisoning and the hanging perhaps,—he concluded that the end justified the means. For this man loved his countrymen and sought their good, though at the time they knew it not. " Willie and myself did the best day's work of our lives," he told his wife when he walked into his house an hour later. And Willie, as he trotted home beside his father, who had relieved him of the basket, thought he understood what the factor meant when he said, " Gad, I have it ! " When late at night they reached their home, they found Shine almost distracted with terror. When she saw Ian coming in, she threw herself on his breast, and with her arms clinging round his neck she kissed him, saying, " Thank God, thank God, you are safe." And when Willie had gone to bed, she came softly to him and said, " You will never do a better deed than you have done to-day, my boy, for you have, perhaps, saved your father's life." And Willie dreamed of Mr. Alastair standing with his cigarette facing the crowd on the hill, and he awoke with a scream as he heard the shouts, " To the river with him; the water will cool the devil in the red factor."

· **THE END.**

MᴇᴛʜᴜEɴ & ᴄᴏᴍᴘᴀɴʏ
ᴀEW YORK.

s.b.